For William,

There will be times when you just want to sit back and be comforted by a good book. This is that kind of book. Hope you enjoy it — and think of your friends in Indiana.

The Herrins

Bayou Bill's Best Stories

Bayou Bill's
Best Stories

BILL SCIFRES

Indiana University Press
BLOOMINGTON AND INDIANAPOLIS

The paper used in this publication meets the minimum requirements of American
National Standard for Information Sciences—Permanence of Paper for Printed
Library Materials, ANSI Z39.48-1984.

Manufactured in the United States of America

Library of Congress Cataloging-in-Publication Data

Scifres, Bill
    Bayou Bill's best stories / Bill Scifres.
      p.   cm.
    ISBN 0-253-35059-X (alk. paper). — ISBN 0-253-30596-4 (pbk. :
alk. paper)
    1. Outdoor life—Fiction. 2. Outdoor life—Indiana. 3. Indiana—
Fiction.   I. Title II. Title: Best stories.
    PS3569.C575B39 1990
    814'.54—dc20   89-78533
                                                            CIP

1 2 3 4 5 94 93 92 91 90

cat—and followed the interloper behind the building. I expected a minor explosion, but there were no sounds at all. Less than a minute later the dog retreated to the house, his tail between his legs. I stopped at the farmhouse and gained permission from the farmer to stalk the badger with my camera, but I could find no trace of the animal.

My only other experience with a badger in the "wilds" of Indiana had come on a Saturday evening in downtown Indianapolis. I had left my office to go for lunch at a little restaurant on the near northside and was returning to work about 9:30 P.M. on Pennsylvania Street in an early December snow. The badger was running on the sidewalk along what was then a parking lot where the new federal building now stands on the east side of Pennsylvania.

I did not tell anybody about that experience for many years because I was not sure I could believe what I had seen. But the animal showed all the characteristics—including the slinky, belly-to-the-ground movement—of the badger I later saw while fishing. I might add that I am not a drinking man.

In the column I recounted my experiences with the blooming water willow, the turtle-shaped rocks, the elusive badger and some other finds of the day. In concluding it, I referred tongue-in-cheek to my fishing adventure as a "bad day" because the fishing had been so slow. The copyreader used that theme in the headline, which was sizable.

A few days later an envelope arrived at the office from fellow outdoor writer Al Spiers of Michigan City. It contained only a tearsheet of my column with a note scribbled across the top. "Bad day, your sweet bippy!" the message read, to paraphrase it somewhat. "You had the time of your life!" And so I did.

That, in my opinion, is what the out-of-doors is all about. If you can find something to enjoy on the bad days out there in the boonies, you will go home from every excursion with a reward. It may not be the thing you went after, but it still will be something of value, perhaps a memory to cherish for the remainder of a lifetime.

Sure, I thrill when a flock of wood ducks flush so close that I can see drops of water falling off their bodies, and it never is easy to forget the tail-walking antics of a husky smallmouth bass. Nor is the ultimate goal of my efforts—the table values—of any less import.

Still, not even the life of the best-informed and most woodsy person on earth can be sun-to-sun sequences of such adventures. There must be those times between shots, strikes and other exciting occurrences. If these times can be used to study or observe the total outdoors, a person will profit in many ways. These secondary encounters with nature can be like spreading a euchre hand to find a brace of lonesome aces when you already knew you held both bowers and the ace of trumps.

If one gets to the point where secondary encounters with nature gain any measure of importance in one's overall outdoor philosophy, there will be times when primary and secondary experiences clash. When this occurs, a person's cup of outdoor pleasure runneth over.

True, I go forth with rod, gun and a variety of other paraphernalia with a purpose of enjoying a hunting or fishing experience and bringing back something for the table. But if these efforts are somehow thwarted, I usually find something else to charge against the day.

Robert Louis Stevenson may not have been thinking of outdoor pleasures when he penned his "Happy Thought." But it still flits through my mind often when nature parades a phalanx of flora and fauna across my outdoor proscenium:

> The world is so full of a number of things,
> I'm sure we should all be as happy as kings.

There is, it seems to me, much more to being an outdoorsman—or an outdoorswoman, of course—than hunting and fishing. I also believe that if you develop this theme to the next plateau you will place all forms of life on the same level.

Few assign the same value to the English sparrow and the bobwhite quail, a magnificent buck deer and a lowly mole, or to many other species of animal life—even plants— which leave contrary impressions. Yet the person who can appreciate the evil and ugly in nature as much as the useful and beautiful is on the path to total enjoyment of the outdoors.

On a summer night a few years back, the members of our family registered varying opinions—even fears—about the storm that raged outside. As I sat near the picture window, jagged flashes of lightning made it possible to see the punishment being dished out by the elements. But in spite of my concern for our trees and other possessions—including the house—the words of some simple verses kept running through my mind. Finally I went to the den and jotted them down on a piece of paper:

> I love the earth in sunshine bright;
> I love it in the dark of night.
> I love it when the raindrops fall;
> Oh, yes, dear God, I love it all!

This book is a collection of stories about my experiences with nature. Although the stories were selected more or less at random, they span more than half a century and I like to think that each of the experiences has in some way contributed to the way I feel about what many folks refer to as "the great outdoors." There have been many other experiences, but as the years have passed the experiences related here have come to mind more often than the others. That has gained them a place in this book.

Incidentally, as the chapters of this book were taking shape, I noticed something which I think is noteworthy. By the time I was halfway home in the pleasant task of writing the various chapters, it became obvious that the stories were either light, happy experiences—with yours truly often being the goatish victim of nature or a companion—or they were sad, even dramatic. Some, of course, have elements of both. These are my favorites.

I have learned much—and continue to learn—about nature, but if I had to choose the one most important thing I have gained from these associations, it would be the ability to laugh at myself. If a man can laugh at himself, it does not hurt nearly so much when he is laughed at by others.

At this juncture, then, as author of this book, I would have two wishes. The first would be that you, the reader, will find the same satisfaction in the out-of-doors that I have found, and in the same manner. The second would be that you will enjoy my stories.

Bayou Bill's Best Stories

The Whys and Wherefores
of Bayou Bill and Family

It takes a heap o' livin' in a house t' make it home,
A heap o' sun an' shadder, an' ye sometimes have t' roam,
Afore ye really 'preciate the thing ye lef' behind,
An' hunger fer 'em somehow, with 'em allus on yer mind.
                                                    —Edgar A. Guest

HOW A LITTLE PIECE of Hamilton County, Indiana, came
to be my changing world is a story in itself. As a matter
of fact, if I tell the story right here at the outset, some
of my other stories may be better understood.

When I came to the *Indianapolis Star* as a police reporter
in the winter of 1953, my humble abode—and that is not
a bad adjective—was a downtown apartment.

As chance would have it, the *Star* had an opening for an outdoor writer less than a month after my arrival, and one of my bosses, Jim Farmer (then assistant city editor), suggested that I might want to take on the job.

I checked it out with Sports Editor Jep Cadou, Jr., and he said I could audition for the job by writing a sample column. That first effort as a columnist was published on January 21, 1954.

Farmer, incidentally, was as clever and witty as sin itself, and he became the perpetrator of many a joke, with yours truly always wearing the goat horns. On the day my first column appeared in the paper there was a telegram waiting when I arrived late in the afternoon for work.

It read: "CONGRATULATIONS NEW OUTDOOR COLUMN. GREAT STUFF. I'D RATHER WRITE THAN BE PRESIDENT."

It was signed Dwight D. Eisenhower.

My first thought, while standing at my mailbox, was "How'd he know about that so soon?"

Then I saw Jim at his desk with that "I didn't do nothin'" grin on his face.

I still have to chuckle when the telegram turns up among my treasures.

My police reporting duties continued, of course—the column, which appeared twice weekly for a few months and three times weekly since, being only a part-time job. My path at the *Star* eventually led to the copy desk and on to a position known as "makeup editor." With my column always appearing in the sports section, however, I eventually gravitated to that department.

In the meantime, the spring of 1954 came on schedule— the world continued to revolve in spite of the deathless prose and poetry I turned out for columns—and in April of that year I conned Miss Nancy C. Wellington into letting me put an engagement ring on her finger.

Anticipating the fall nuptials—conducted on the following September 4 at Northminster Presbyterian Church—I moved into a nifty little third-floor (no elevator) apartment at 13th and Pennsylvania Streets. In the interim Nancy would bring her father and mother (Lucile and Paul Wellington) up to the place to paint and do other chores so it would be shipshape when we were wed.

Thus, when we returned from our honeymoon trip to the coast of Maine, where we (mostly I) caught a number of ocean species of fish—including Spanish mackerel (very tasty when broiled)—we were able to get going with our lives without having to track down an apartment, no easy chore in those days.

Nancy, who had majored in chemistry at Knox College in Illinois, worked for Eli Lilly and Company in a testing laboratory until the first of our three daughters, Donna, was born five years later. We wanted children from the start, but that is not the way it happened. As a matter of fact, No. 2 daughter, Joan, did not arrive until Donna was seven years old, and Patricia would wind up the parade two years after that.

Nancy worked days and I worked nights. We would have Sundays and a few rare Saturdays to do as we liked, but on the other days we would meet at a downtown restaurant for supper before I went to work. We would not see each other again until 2:00 or later the following morning, when the *Star's* city edition rolled off the presses and operations were temporarily suspended.

To further complicate our lives, I did not own an automobile. Thus, if I wanted to go fishing or hunting while she worked on a weekday, I would take her to work early in the morning and would be back (on a high percentage of these occasions) in time to pick her up when she got off work at 4:30 P.M.

I say I would be back "on a high percentage of these occasions" because there were a few times when I was late—

and maybe one or two times when I did not make it at all. The results were always the same. The feathers flew.

Take, for example, this one beautiful late April day when I was off on Wednesday after working the police beat until 2:00 A.M. I wanted to wade the Big Blue River downstream from Shelbyville for smallmouth in the worst way, even though I had gotten little sleep and still was tired. I wrapped up a couple of sandwiches and an apple, dropped Nancy off at work with the promise to be punctual on my return, and headed for the river with my waders and fishing tackle.

The water was still cold, but the sun was warm and bright. When I crawled up on a small, willow-infested island in the middle of the creek about noon to test my culinary skills, I found a beautiful little clearing covered with warm, dry, fluffy sand.

About the time I polished off the apple for dessert I noticed a pair of yellow-shafted flickers going through their premating ritual, high on a beech limb in the adjacent woods. They sat face to face on the limb—probably ten inches apart—and moved their heads from side to side in unison. It was a strange but interesting performance.

I became so engrossed in the proceedings that in a few minutes my neck became sore from looking upward and the thought struck like a bolt out of the blue: I could watch the birds just as well—and be more comfortable—if I would lie on my back in the sand. With the warm sand on my back and the bright sun caressing my full belly, I soon pulled the battered old cap down over my eyes to blot out the sun and the birds, and soon I was in never-never land.

You know the rest of the story. Things were testy that night.

We liked living downtown, but we started looking for a house almost immediately. One of the first houses we looked at was situated on the east bank of White River's West Fork just south of 116th Street—a small residential area with the river on one side and farm fields on the other. It was and still is known as Trail's End.

This little house, which we purchased and sold some fourteen years later for less than many Chevies and Fords go for today, was of cinder block exterior and had been constructed in the middle of several large maple, elm, hackberry and sycamore trees. It had a large living room with fireplace and windows looking out over the river on either side. It also had a small kitchen and dining area bisected by a two-stool eating bar, and the old crank telephone was attached to the wall there.

There were two large bedrooms and one small bedroom which became my den and workroom. Then, of course, there was a comfortable bathroom and a garage large enough to house one automobile and all the junk we accumulated in the next fourteen years.

We first saw the place late on a Sunday afternoon. Nancy had noticed the small classified ad telling about the property, and we couldn't wait for an appointment to see it. We drove out, arriving just before dark. We couldn't go in, but as we drove slowly past, there were a number of lights on inside the house and everyplace we looked we saw knotty pine. We were sold right there.

We moved in on July 5—it was a lot easier than when we moved out—and if we liked the place when we first saw it, it wasn't long before we loved it. Why wouldn't we like it? There was the hoot of owls at night instead of the screaming sirens of police cars, ambulances and fire trucks; the pleasing aroma of farm fields, freshly plowed ground and the river instead of the city dump; mink, muskrat, waterfowl and a blue zillion other children of nature instead of people.

Little wonder that I would wax poetic at times when I was writing a column—even if the sports editor did not always appreciate my efforts.

One time, for example, Mother Nature's critters interrupted my thoughts so often as I whacked out a Sunday column on my beat-up old Royal that I started dropping couplets in between items—even between paragraphs of items.

The years have erased the column items, but some of the couplets are still etched indelibly in my mind.

Frankly, I think the slot man who laid out the paper that Sunday did a great job with the column. He set the type two columns wide, as I recall, displaying the column items in regular roman body type with my couplets set in a font of lightface italic.

As I say, I do not remember any of the column items, but now and then one of the couplets will haunt me when I am musing over the past. For example:

Ol' kingfisher, 'cross the river, strikes a pose nor any quiver,
Doesn't even seem to shiver when he dives in near the ice.

Then there was:

Little ol' brown creeper, he—sneaks on up yon dead elm tree,
Pickin' things that you and me never would have eyes to see.

The theme of the column revolved around the fact that I was aware that I had my reportorial duties to complete but that Mother Nature kept interfering, and that I hoped the readers would bear with me in this thing.

Folks loved it. Well, most folks. The sports editor left a note in my mailbox which said, in effect: "That will be enough of your doggerel!"

I found his note rather amusing until I looked up *doggerel* in the dictionary. What the heck, I never had considered myself a Riley or a Kipling. I just liked to put things down on paper that rhymed and sounded nice.

At any rate, since that time I have strived to keep my

verse and poems from creeping into my columns and other prose. But I am not always successful.

I tell you these things to make one point. Living on Trail's End was all an outdoorsman could hope for. No matter what I was doing—writing a column, raking leaves, painting the house, cleaning the gutters or any one of a hundred other chores a homeowner must take care of—I could always count on old Ma Nature to provide a respite, at times a diversion.

But even at that, it was obvious to me—right from the start—that we would someday have to leave this most peaceful of places to live. I knew that I would have to give up going in and out by boat when the river would rise in the spring; that I might someday have to live at a place where I could not talk with the hoot owls when I got home from work in the wee hours of the morning or at a place where I could not look out across flooded fields to see great blue herons or hear the call of the bobwhite quail.

I knew it because Nancy, who had always wanted to be an architect but was guided into chemistry instead, was continually designing our dream house.

Thus I was not surprised a few short years later when she started coming home and telling me that she had noticed an interesting classified ad in the paper about a piece of land—with or without house—for sale somewhere around the north side of Indianapolis in Marion, Boone or Hamilton Counties.

"Well," I would always say, "we can go look at it, but I'll tell you before we go: it is going to have to be something special to get me to leave this river."

I must have sounded like a broken record on that matter. A man can become more than a little attached to a house on a river if he sees and hears and smells and senses the things I learned to love on Trail's End. Anyhow, I liked the idea of having a telephone on the Fishers exchange.

We looked at two or three log cabins, wooded acreage and just about everything else Nancy thought might lure me away from the river, but it was always the same. I would take one look at these places and announce staidly: "I wouldn't leave the river for this!"

Yes, a man can get mighty attached to a place when he can look out his den window and see a smallmouth bass jump. Or a mink, a muskrat, a pied-billed grebe or a flock of goldeneye. I'll tell you, it is easy.

After about twelve years on the river, Nancy announced one day that there was a piece of land for sale on 111th Street between Carmel and Indianapolis. The kids—by then we had Donna and Joan—would go to the Carmel schools, she said, but the property was not in the town.

"Oh, yes!" she said, as if she had almost forgotten about it. "There's a natural pond and lots of trees."

We drove over to look at the place on a Sunday afternoon in the early fall in spite of my grousing that we probably were on another of Nancy's wild goose chases. There was no driveway into the property, so we parked along the side of 111th Street as best we could (not much traffic there on a Sunday afternoon in those days) and started walking leisurely back to the pond.

I noticed signs of squirrels working on beechnuts as we walked under two large beech trees, and I saw muskrat signs at the edge of the pond. I had seen and heard several kinds of birds, including a green heron, before we slipped through the screen of white pines at the north end of the pond and walked up the slight rise, where several large beech, poplar and ash trees and one little white oak dwelled.

Just as we reached the top of the rise a covey of quail exploded, and when we had calmed down I think my first words were "It would be a shame, but we would have to cut at least one of these big beech trees to put a house up here."

So it was.

We owned the property two years before we finally built Nancy's house.

The winter Nancy was pregnant with Patty was cold, and the place on Trail's End wasn't the warmest house you ever saw.

"I don't want to spend another winter in this house," Nancy said, emphatically.

"Well," said I, "take your house plans to John Polley (a builder with whom I had gone to high school at Crothersville) and get some blueprints made. John probably can build us a house there next spring."

That's the way it happened, but not without a hitch or two, the two most important ones revolving around a beech tree where the driveway should have entered the property and the little white oak on the hill.

I was there bright and early on the morning construction was to start, and the first thing John told me was that it appeared as though the big beech near the road would have to go to make room for the driveway.

"It looks to me like the driveway could be slipped in there without cutting the old beech," I countered, but John came back with the startling fact that trucks hauling in materials would have trouble getting in.

"The tree stays," I said, then asked a question I knew he would answer favorably: "If you can't get the materials in there, you can't build a house, can you?"

I left him there to ponder my question.

Some of the top of the beech is gone now, some twenty years later, but the tree still stands, a living smorgasbord for every species of woodpecker found in Indiana, including a pair of pileateds. I figure that vindicates my stern stand on the issue.

We had a similar problem with the little white oak, then only six inches or so in diameter.

On the day John, Nancy and I staked out the corners of the house, we soon learned that Nancy's creation, a ranch type, would fit nicely on the little hill if we would cut the big beech that stood about where the front door now is situated. We had agreed that we would make that sacrifice. We didn't want to lose the tree, but it was one of those things that had to happen if we were to live there.

Then the shocker came. The county building code would not permit construction within a given distance of the east property line, and that meant the house would be pushed about ten feet to the west and the little white oak also would have to go.

We solved that problem almost before it arose.

"What the heck," we told John, almost in unison. "We will scale all of the rooms down a bit—they still are rather large when compared to most houses—and cut four feet off the length of the house."

The four-foot bulldozer blade scar on the south side of the little white oak has long since healed, and the tree now is roughly fifteen inches in diameter five feet above the ground. More importantly, I can't count the times I have awakened in my bed and looked out the window to see some beautiful bird or animal using the little white oak as a feeding ground or resting place.

If that wildlife menagerie is not enough to make me realize the soundness of our decision on the little white oak, I still have to smile when I consider that we pay no taxes on the four feet of house we did not build.

My Changing World

"HELLO, JACK! YOU THERE?" I said, neither expecting nor getting an answer. "I hope you don't mind if I sit down and visit for a while."

With that I eased down into the grass and weeds at the end of my front-yard pond and peered carefully into the dry leaves at the base of the stump of the little red pine tree.

Two years earlier the red pine, some five inches in diameter, had been part of a most interesting ecosystem which provided some rare experiences with the flora and fauna of my world. And one of the most interesting revolved around the development of Jack—one jack-in-the-pulpit plant.

Jack lived at the base of the pine. I first became aware of his presence on an early fall day as I sat on an old hand-hewn log bench nearby. It was the cluster of fire-engine-red berries—the culmination of a spring and summer's growth—that caught my eye.

I could not have been more pleased to learn that Jack lived there. In my knowledge, he—if one can separate plants by gender—was the only jack-in-the-pulpit in my world, the 1.67-acre plot of land on 111th Street between Carmel and Indianapolis in southern Hamilton County.

Little wonder that I would interrupt my spring yard chores on a bright and warm day late in March to see if he had returned. I knew that sooner or later he would not come back because living conditions no longer were ideal for him there.

For many years the hollow beech tree had leaned out over the south end of the natural pond which had lured me and my family to this beautiful spot. But two years earlier, on a turbid summer day, a tornado had roared through the area at treetop level, and part of the tax nature had levied on my world was the life of this magnificent tree.

For several years I had used the leaning beech, a good three feet in diameter five feet above the ground, to frame pictures I would take of winter scenes on the pond: neighborhood kids skating, or shoveling the snow to keep the ice smooth, that sort of thing. In the summer I would sit on the park bench at the north end of the pond late in the afternoon to watch as a mother raccoon would bring her babies out of their lair high in the hollow of the old tree to "feel" for food in the shallow water of the pond. Now and again our resident pileated woodpecker would visit the tree.

The propensity of the American beech to develop hollow trunks makes this species an ideal den for many species of wild animals because its slick bark makes it difficult for enemies to climb. Raccoons have trouble climbing beech trees because the bark is so slick, and for this reason they often gain access to dens by climbing nearby saplings and crossing over to the sprangling limbs of a beech.

That had been one of the earliest lessons my father, the late Jacob W. Scifres, had taught me about the wild animals and birds which have been so much a part of my life.

We were squirrel hunting on this particular day, but no matter what my dad might be doing outdoors he was never too busy to learn something about wild animals, nor to share his knowledge with me.

"That's a coon den, Bill!" he said emphatically, pointing to a big, smooth-barked beech tree some twenty-five or thirty feet from the spot where he stood at the base of a much smaller tree. So far as I knew, he had never seen these trees before and I wondered how he could know such a thing.

I didn't have to wonder long.

"See the scratches?" he said, pointing to the bark of the small tree where we stood. He explained that the bark of the beech was too slick and too large in diameter (the raccoons couldn't hug it) for coons to climb, so they went up the smaller tree to reach the limbs of the large tree.

Raccoons have no problems climbing most other big trees in Indiana because their bark is rough. The beech is another matter, and coons telegraph their use of such dens by the scratches they put on nearby saplings. They take the same route nearly every time.

This beech tree here in my changing world was different. It must have leaned out over the end of the pond at an angle of at least fifteen or twenty degrees—probably, I theorized, because early in life it had to fight for the life-giving light of the sunshine in a dense hardwood forest. This angle made it easy for a raccoon to climb the tree. At times, when contemplating the beauty of the tree, I fancied that even a man, at least an agile man or a boy, might be able to run right up the side of the tree—if he could get a good start.

High in the top of the tree a four-inch limb had broken off at the point where it joined the trunk of the tree. That had opened up a stovepipelike passage in the massive trunk, and this passage ended at a "room" nearly as big as a bushel basket ten feet below where several large limbs angled out in all directions.

Having never climbed the tree, I did not know these things until I was investigating the havoc wrought upon my little world by this freakish tornado. But as I stood knee-deep in the pond after the storm had passed late in the afternoon and directed the beam of the flashlight into the hollow to see the beady eyes of the mother raccoon and her young in the great room, it became obvious that the old tree had been a wonderful den. I would learn much more about this as I rendered the massive trunk and limbs into fireplace wood.

It was unfortunate, I thought, that the old tree's final hurrah would come so humbly, as smoke going up my fireplace chimney.

More fortunate, at least for the mother raccoon and her babies, was the fact that the same storm which robbed them of their home took out one of the three prongs of another beech tree no more than thirty feet from our front door. In so doing, nature had evened the score in raccoon dens, because when the towering fork split away from the main trunk of the tree near the house, another large cavity was opened to any critter who cared to use it. And it went from the spot where the three prongs of the tree had forked, some thirty feet above the ground, nearly to ground level.

This tree had grown straight and tall—a monarch in what once had undoubtedly been a beautiful beech and hardwood forest—and its sprangling limbs reached out twenty feet or more to a line of white pines to provide ready access, especially to an animal with the den-finding instincts of the raccoon.

So it was that the elements and nature had combined their efforts to move at least a portion of the raccoon populace closer to our picture window. This eventually would pay great dividends for both the members of my family and the raccoons. As a matter of fact, on the day this was written (in late June 1989) my attention was pretty much evenly divided between the newsgatherers on the evening news and a mother raccoon preparing her four fuzzy children for their first trip to terra firma.

More on that later. Now back to Jack.

Although the old leaning beech tree had provided a wonderful place for a mother raccoon and her babies during the summer months and undoubtedly a snug place for many adult animals during the winter months (they tend to congregate in extremely cold weather), other residents of the area were not so fortunate.

What could have told this story more graphically than the space between the limbs that sprangled out from the trunk of the little white pine tree, which had been shaded from—and robbed of—the life-giving rays of the sun by the old leaning beech?

It was all there to see. White pines at other locations on the property showed annual growth rates of eighteen inches to two feet almost every year in the space between limbs. But while this little tree was some ten years old, it was no more than four feet high.

Little wonder that my neighbor approached me one day and asked permission to move the obviously stunted white pine.

"It's never going to do anything there," the well-intentioned neighbor said. "I'll move it to my yard and give it a place to grow, if you don't mind."

I told my neighbor I didn't really mind, but I thought I would like to leave the little pine right where it was.

"You never know what will happen down the road,"

I philosophized. "I think I would like to keep that little tree."

There could be no doubt about it. The passing of the leaning beech was a severe blow to me, my family and many wild birds and animals of the area—its crop of beechnuts in good years provided a bountiful harvest for coons, squirrels and birds. Nor was I averse to tickling my palate with a few beechnut meats now and again. Still, its demise touched off a fantastic growth on the part of the stunted white pine and several other saplings. The canes in the blackberry patch started growing as if there would be no tomorrow.

But I also knew that the same light that brought prosperity to the little white pine and the underbrush of the small area would someday spell doom for Jack. The added sunlight would sap the earth of the moisture the deeply shaded area once held, and one year soon Jack would simply not awaken from his long winter sleep.

"Perhaps this will be the year Jack will not return," I told myself as my fingers slipped softly into the dead leaves and twigs and gently pulled them back from the base of the little red pine stump.

For several seconds I saw nothing, but then my eyes picked up the tiny, cream-colored point of a plant no larger than the head of a kitchen match as it pushed laboriously through the earth to greet the spring.

"Welcome back, Jack!" I said, my fingers gently touching the tiny nodule.

Satisfied that Jack would be with us for at least one more year and knowing that my friend would find his way to sunshine when the threat of frost had passed, I pulled the protective covering of dead leaves and grass back over the spot and entertained thoughts of resuming my work.

About that time my visit with Jack was interrupted by Joan and Patty, who had sauntered down the driveway from the front yard.

"Who you talking to, Daddy?" one of them asked, and for a moment their presence and their question took me more than somewhat aback.

"I guess I was just talking to myself," I said, pulling them both onto my lap as I sat down again on the old hand-hewn log.

Even as I said it I knew that was not right. It didn't even sound right. It was a lie, I told myself, adding that I shouldn't be lying to my daughters—not even if it were a little white lie.

"No!" I told them, after thinking it over. "I wasn't talking to myself. I was talking to a jack-in-the-pulpit—it's a wildflower that grows right there." I pointed to the base of the red pine stump, then scooted back there on hands and knees to uncover Jack again so they could see for themselves.

I explained how in the coming days the plant would push its cream-colored spike up through the leaves and how it would turn into an olive-splotched stem a foot or less tall with a single spread of three leaves; how it would be topped by a small, pale green (perhaps even striped) tubular vaselike swelling (the pulpit) with pointed hood protecting the small sticklike Jack which would grow inside.

"It'll look like a little preacher in a pulpit," I said, continuing that the little preacher would develop into a cluster of fifteen or twenty closely bunched green berries through the summer and the thin skin of the pulpit would peel away, leaving the cluster of berries perched on top of the stem.

The berries, I told them, would turn fire-engine red early in the fall and would be eaten by birds and chipmunks and otherwise scattered to the far corners of our little world—perhaps even farther—and that some of the seeds probably would produce more plants to preserve the species, even if our resident Jack should someday give up the ghost.

That appeared to satisfy the inquisitive minds of my daughters. But the next day at work I related the experience to a couple of friends in the coin cafeteria. There was more than a little eyeball rolling between the two when I got to the part about talking to Jack.

"I always knew you were a little flaky," said one of my friends as they walked away. "Now we know it," the other chimed in.

"Tell you what," I said as a parting shot. "If you won't tell your friends I talk to wildflowers and critters, I won't tell my friends that you don't!"

B-A-R-U-M-P-H!
One Fine Father's Day Present

IT WAS HOT! No, it wasn't just hot. It was "hotter'n blue
blazes," as daughter Patty put it—quoting my Crothers-
villese—when she came out the front door to find me putting
together some beehives.

"Yes, it is," I said, confirming her comment on the
weather. "Tonight would be a good time to go frog hunting,"
I continued, adding that the season for frog hunting had
opened the night before at midnight.

"Can we go, Dad?" she asked.

"Why not?" I said. "We can do what we want to do
this weekend."

My wife, Nancy, and daughter Joan were off on a tennis
junket to South Carolina, and the schedule of older daughter

Donna would not conflict. We could do as we pleased, but at the moment I rather doubted that we would go frog hunting. A sixteen-year-old girl doesn't usually get real excited about being in muck up to her knees on a hot and dark night. Most girls of this age would not even consider grabbing a slimy frog with their bare hands.

I busied myself with working the bees, mowing the lawn and doing several other chores through the hot June afternoon, and Patty presented me with my Father's Day present which the girls had gotten earlier in the week. I can't remember now what it was—maybe a shirt or a jug of Old Spice—but I am sure I was sincere when I told Patty it was very nice.

Late in the afternoon Patty suggested we go to the Steak 'N Shake for supper, and it was getting dark when we got back home to feed the cats, dogs and raccoons and finish up the other chores. But eventually I turned on the TV—there didn't seem to be much else to do—and started to rev it down for the night.

That didn't last long.

Patty appeared in the doorway to the living room with a question: "Can we go, Dad? Can we go frog hunting?"

"Why not?" I said again, and started giving her instructions about wearing old clothes and other such matters.

In less than ten minutes we were headed for a farm pond only a few miles from home with flashlight, burlap bag, cameras and other paraphernalia.

We had to park a quarter of a mile or so from the pond and walk through a woods to get there, so we were wringing wet with sweat by the time we arrived.

At the edge of the pond we stopped and I turned off the light. Patty wanted to talk, but I shushed her.

"Listen!" I said. "Maybe we'll hear our first customer."

For what seemed an eternity we heard several sounds of the night—the hoot of an owl and the bark of a dog in the distance, and some unidentifiable pond critters—but no frogs.

"Maybe there aren't any frogs here," Patty said. This notion was dispelled by the hearty "B-A-R-U-M-P-H, B-A-R-U-M-P-H" of a frog so close that Patty was a little shaken.

"Stay right behind me," I said, slipping through the brush and stepping into the edge of the pond, which was bordered by cattails and a mixture of other aquatic weeds and sported six or eight inches of black muck on its bottom.

I eased into the cattails until I was knee-deep, then turned on the light and swept the shoreline ahead with its beam. For a few seconds there was nothing but weeds, but twelve or fifteen feet ahead two small bright spots showed in the beam of the light and we could pick out the body of the frog—a good one.

"You watch me catch this one," I told Patty, "then we'll take turns."

With that I started my move on the frog, explaining each thing I did in minute detail: "Once I get the beam of the light in the frog's eyes, it is kept there until I make my grab," I said, moving in slowly from a spot directly in front of the frog. "This keeps the light in both eyes of the frog and it is blinded."

As I neared the frog I dropped down to my knees in the muck and explained that I would lean in with the light (in my left hand) no more than four or five inches from the frog's nose. From there I would reach around from the side with my right hand to grab the frog firmly just behind the front legs.

"When you make the grab it must be fast and firm," I cautioned. "Touch the frog or cause a stick or blade of grass to touch it, and it will jump into the water and escape."

I couldn't have done it any better. I made the grab and came up with the frog in one smooth motion that brought one word from Patty: "Wow!"

With that frog in the wet burlap bag which was tied to my waist, I took time out to explain to Patty the reasons for catching frogs with the hands instead of shooting them with bird shot in a .22-caliber rifle or gigging (spearing) them.

"Catch 'em with your hands," I explained, "and you can release them later if you don't get enough for a frog dinner. If you shoot them or gig them, they're dead."

With that I shined the light down the bank and the beam picked up another bright spot—another frog.

"He's a big one," Patty said. "Let me catch him."

Patty took the light and I readied my camera for the action.

She made a beautiful approach on the frog, even though the water in front of her quarry was a little deeper than she had anticipated. When she was three or four feet away from the frog she dropped to her knees and scooted in until the light was almost on the frog's nose. Slowly her right hand came around and with a lightninglike stab she grabbed the frog and jumped to her feet with water and mud flying in all directions.

Patty was mud from head to toe, but she hoisted the monstrous bullfrog over her head and yelled, "I got 'im, Dad!"

Indeed, she had.

I let Patty do most of the catching the rest of the night. I offered suggestions now and then, but otherwise I let her do her thing. On one occasion there was a bodacious frog sitting back under a large clump of willows which bent low over the water to create a space barely large enough to crawl into. She had to half crawl, half slither nearly ten feet through slimy muck with her back raking the willows above about half the time.

She didn't get that one—I think she may have allowed the light to waver off the frog just before she made her grab, and it bounced off her arms when it jumped. The fact that Patty had missed the frog was of no consequence. I doubted that I could have caught it. Of greater importance was the fact that Patty had not hesitated to go in that snake den after the frog, even though the place would have made me think twice.

We kept only four of the frogs we caught—Patty's first frog, which we named Margaret, and three others. All were released in our pond.

It was past midnight when we got back home that night. While we were enjoying a bedtime snack in the living room, Patty asked me a question: "Did you like your Father's Day present?"

"It was the best I ever had," I said.

Afterthought: Margaret provided sweet music from our pond on hot nights the rest of that summer and most of the next. Eventually, though, she either died of old age or fell prey to another of nature's children—perhaps a raccoon. But now that the pond provides much better habitat for frogs, it would not be at all surprising if Patty and I should take another frog hunt before this book is published and that we hear the "B-A-R-U-M-P-H, B-A-R-U-M-P-H" of Margaret II on hot, dark nights. It makes a super lullaby.

Margaret was not the first resident bullfrog of our front-yard pond.

As mentioned in a previous chapter, we purchased the property on 111th Street some two years before we built our present house, and while we still lived on the river we visited the pond and trees often. We were putting down some roots.

It was late winter when we decided to build the new house on the little rise behind the pond, and construction was started late in the spring. The builders had made good progress by the middle of June, and while I could not spend a lot of time watching, Nancy was there often.

Soon after the frog season opened early in the summer I had gone frog hunting with Woody Fleming, then the director of the Division of Fish and Wildlife, and brought home a burlap bag of frogs. One was a real monster.

It was almost daylight when I got home, so I just wet the burlap bag down with the garden hose and stashed the frogs in the shade of a shrub at the side of the house.

Of course, Nancy asked what I was going to do with the frogs. I informed her that I would "clean" them when I got up that day and wondered would she turn on the hose now and again and wet the burlap bag down to keep the frogs comfy.

She wet them down, all right. But she also looked into the bag and took a liking to that big frog.

Later in the morning she headed for the new house and thought she might just as well take that big frog over to the pond and turn him loose.

She placed the frog in another bag, which she put on the floor of the T-Bird for the trip to the new house, but she hadn't much more than left the old house before the frog pulled a Houdini and was jumping all over the car.

Nancy had the windows of the car rolled down because it did not offer the luxury of air conditioning, but she stopped and rolled the windows up and sweated it out the rest of the way.

The frog was jumping at the windows—they must have looked like freedom—and other motorists were having a ball at the stoplights and on the road as Nancy suffered through her plight. When she told the story I surmised that if one has not had to dodge a jumping bullfrog in traffic, one has not lived.

The frog finally found a secluded spot under the front seat and was still hiding there when Nancy arrived at the new house.

Nancy asked the contractor if he would help her put the frog in the pond, but he took one look at the size of the frog and said no thanks. She finally pulled the frog out by the legs and marched to the pond with it. The contractor went about the business of building our house, but not without looking over his shoulder and scratching his head.

I must admit to having designs on that big bullfrog's hammy back legs, but when I heard the story later in the day, I quickly concluded that one frog—even one very big frog—probably would be lonesome in the pond. So I took him some company. Still, we had a bait of fried froglegs at our house.

One of the most interesting frog-hunting experiences I ever had came on a hot, humid and very dark August night on the East Fork of the Muscatatuck River upstream from what was then the Slate Ford Bridge.

A sizable crowd of kids my age were camping in an old tin-roofed shanty, and Jack Cain had joined us. I can't remember exactly who made the froggin' trip, but I do know Jack was there as sort of a guide and Lloyd Meeks was along. Altogether, though, there were four or five of us in an old wood boat.

We could hear a humongous frog down the river a hundred yards or more, and Jack told us about a frog that several people had heard on this stretch of the river. Nobody had been able to catch the frog, Jack told us, adding that if we were cautious maybe we could.

Jack said the frog lived in the root wad of a big maple tree that had been deposited in this deep hole by floodwaters.

"Let's turn out the lights and keep real quiet until we are right there by the roots," he said. "Maybe we can catch him."

It never is easy to keep three or four teen-age boys quiet anywhere—in a boat on a hot, dark night is no different. So there was some whispering and snickering as the boat drifted silently toward the root wad. It was a rare experience.

Without the lights we all acquired a certain amount of night vision, and as we drew abreast of the big root wad all was quiet. The plan was to sit there with the boat right next to the roots until the frog spoke, then turn the lights in his eyes. Once we had the lights in his eyes we would have a shot at him.

Someone reached out and grabbed a root to keep us there. For what seemed like a very long time there was no noise at all. I could hear someone breathing.

Then the frog cut loose with a gigantic bellow: "B-A-R-U-M-P-H! B-A-R-U-M-P-H!"

The call came with such force that I fancied my ears ached, and maybe they did. But however loud it may have been, we all were taken so much aback that we failed to turn the lights on for several seconds and when the roots and bank finally were swept by the flashlight beams there was nothing to see. No sign of a frog.

We turned the lights out and sat there for half an hour or more, but the frog never barked again.

Many years later I realized that the largest frog I ever saw, I didn't see at all.

A Smorgasbord
of Turtle Stories

To BEGIN WITH, I think it would be well to say that turtles—mainly hardshells (snappers) and softshells (leatherbacks)—have been a source of food and amusement, even consternation, to me for many years.

Take, for example, the warm September day a few years back when I went to southern Indiana to get a load of slab wood for the winter and, later in the day, to work in some gray squirrel hunting in the hill country or to do some fishing on farm ponds or by wading a stream.

I accomplished the first purpose of my trip by a little after noon. The bed of my old Chevy pickup was so full of slabs that I could not close the tailgate.

Then it was off to the farm ponds, but on this warm,

sunny day the fishing was slow. Thus by midafternoon I was driving the back roads to this little hill woods of my acquaintance where I would undoubtedly stay until darkness drove me out.

I rounded a bend in the road and there he was—a snapping turtle that measured seven or eight inches across the back. He was humping down the middle of the road as if he knew precisely where he was going.

I knew the scenario. The dry weather of late summer and early fall had lowered the water level where he lived and he was trying to find more water. He had taken the path of least resistance—the road.

"Hello, Big Boy," I said, pulling abreast and stopping my truck smack in the middle of the road. "How would you like to be the resident snapper in my pond?"

Mr. Meanmouth did not answer my question, but that was of little consequence. The die had been cast the second I saw him. So far as I could tell, my pond did not host any snapping turtles—at least I never had seen one there—and I figured it could stand a few.

The turtle stood his ground and made a menacing hissing sound as I approached, but I managed to grab him by the tail—and there my problems began to mount. I couldn't put him in the truck bed with the wood because I could not close the tailgate. That left only one place—the cab of the truck. The turtle would be a first-class passenger.

With the turtle on the floorboard of the truck in a little pen I fashioned from my chainsaw, axe and a few other items, I continued my trip to the squirrel woods. Things did not go well. The pen did not contain this sojourner's desire to keep moving, and soon he had climbed up on the seat with me and was headed in my direction with blood in his eyes.

After several stops to return the turtle to his own little area, it became evident that more permanent and confining quarters would have to be found. And there it was—the glove compartment.

It was a tight fit, but I managed to get the turtle in and closed the door. It worked to perfection, but there was one small problem. At the squirrel woods the windows of the truck would have to be rolled up, and it could get hot in there. "Maybe," I thought, "the turtle should have free run of the cab until I return."

When I opened to door to the glove compartment, the turtle was not there.

This puzzled me more than a little for a few minutes, but with the fire wall behind the engine of the truck, I knew the turtle had to be under the dash—in there with all the wiring and other good things that make pickup trucks run— and my find quickly took on the image of the proverbial bull in a china closet. Still, I knew the matter was out of my hands. I would just have to take the truck over to Manford and Lester, my neighborhood mechanics, and hope they could take the time to get the turtle out.

I knew I could depend on Manford and Lester—they always straightened out my Mr. Fixit blunders (like the stick in the carburetor that made the motor race out of control when I started the engine). But how would I explain a snapping turtle under the dash?

"Well," I told myself, "I am here to hunt squirrels, not worry about turtles, and I had better do it." At that point my luck took a turn for the better. Not only did the day give me a tremendous final three hours in the woods (including three young gray squirrels), but when I returned to the truck the turtle not only had found his way out of his dashboard prison but also had succeeded in getting a front leg hopelessly entangled in the handle of my chain saw.

"That looks like a good place for you," I told the turtle as I turned the ignition and the motor responded with a roar that left no doubt that all was still in order under the dash. "You can ride right there on the way to your new home."

"And that, my friends, you may think was that, but it wasn't . . . not by a fisherman's hat," if I may pilfer some Ogden Nash. My troubles with that snapper—and some others—were just starting. Still, I would protect him, and some others, to the end, even if it made me look like the original Hard-Hearted Hannah.

Actually, soon after my resident turtle was released in the front-yard pond, I started seeing signs of other snappers there. I could but presume that either the presence of the turtle I brought in or the mere presence of my pond itself had lured in the other turtles when their resident potholes had dried up.

Whatever the rationale, I had at least three snapping turtles in my pond, and it was a joy to sit on the park bench and watch them.

I fetched in road-killed rabbits and squirrels for the turtles to eat, and all went well.

Watching a snapper hide in the aquatic weeds and run that long neck up to the surface of the water to breathe through nostrils which barely broke the surface of the water, seeing a snapper awaken in the mucky shallows after a winter of hibernation, and observing dozens of other strange behavioral patterns were just about all one could ask. I marveled at the ways of nature.

My wife, Nancy, and daughters were not overly concerned about the presence of the snappers in the pond until the hen mallard showed up one day with seven fuzzy little babies, which quickly became the darlings of just about everybody who saw them, including yours truly.

Ma Mallard would gather her brood on a pile of cattail stalks I had pulled up, and if heat, cold or rain threatened their welfare she would spread her wings and the babies would take refuge near her body. It was nature viewing at its best.

One morning, however, someone noticed that there were only six babies, and that brought on a search of the pond area by the girls. That seventh little ball of fuzz had disappeared almost as if it were one of Riley's "Squidgicum-Squees 'at swallers the'rselves."

A day or two later one leg of one of the babies hung limp, and when we captured the little critter it was obvious that something with powerful jaws had done the damage.

The turtles! They were the culprits, I was told by the girls. Then I was ordered to get out my trusty squirrel rifle and eliminate the turtles.

It was difficult to defend the turtles—the only thing I could say was that they were only doing their thing.

The situation got even worse when the crippled little duck died and still another disappeared to bring Ma Mallard's family down to four.

Fortunately, the hen mallard solved the problem. She simply took the remainder of her brood somewhere else.

The turtles were spared, and so was I.

I have since learned that turtles—like other antagonists in the eternal drama of the natural world—get their lumps in many ways.

One of the turtles of my pond liked to lie in ambush under my little jon boat. The boat's bow usually was pulled up onto the bank and created a nifty place where the turtle and other denizens could hide. The angled clay bottom of the pond was almost like rock because I had scooped out the muck. The turtle, I figured, crawled into the place to wait for bluegills, frogs and other critters which took refuge there from the sun.

Many times I would touch the boat lightly, or jiggle it ever so slightly, to see the turtle streak back to deep water.

A snapper, incidentally, can move faster than one might think, either in the water or out.

At any rate, a few days after a toad-strangling rain, I detected a strange odor around the boat, which had been more than half filled by the rain. At first I didn't connect the odor with anything, but one day, as the odor seemed to be getting stronger, I decided to dip the water out of the boat and see what was there.

When I had dipped out enough water to handle the boat, I turned it over to find the turtle dead—obviously the victim of the heavy rain. As the boat filled with water the turtle had been pinned solidly to the bottom.

A closer inspection revealed that the turtle had tried to dig its way out with all four legs, but the mound of clay about the size of the turtle's body had kept it trapped.

It was not a happy day in my world.

Now and then Mother Nature shows an outdoorsman something special, and that is the way it was on an early June afternoon in 1982 as I waded and fished a small stream in northern Indiana.

As I crept through dense brush near a horseshoe bend in the stream, I saw what I first thought was a gigantic softshell turtle on the far bank of the stream. When my binoculars were focused, the turtle turned into a very large snapper, probably fourteen to sixteen inches across the back and weighing more than twenty pounds.

The turtle was fifteen or twenty feet from the edge of the stream on a sand-clay bank that angled up at least thirty or forty feet at twenty-five to thirty-five degrees. For a moment I wondered what the turtle was doing there, but a good stalk got me within sixty feet of the turtle and that, coupled with the picture offered by the little binoculars, made it clear that I was about to be treated to one of nature's dramas—a female snapping turtle digging a hole and depositing her eggs.

I didn't know how long this operation would take, but I did know that I had just walked into Mother Nature's outdoor theater and would be there until the fat lady sang. The fact that there probably would be no more fishing on this day did not cross my mind.

Watching a large hardshell turtle dig a hole and deposit her eggs may not sound like the most exciting thing an outdoorsman has ever done, but in nearly half a century of walking creek banks and wading streams, it was something I had never seen before.

I didn't have a watch that day—knowing the time when one is fishing is a waste of time—but I estimated the whole show must have covered something like three hours. For a good hour, perhaps longer, the big turtle dredged out an almost perfectly round hole in the wet clay-sand mixture with her back legs and feet, working first with one foot while the other leg and tail braced her rear end. Then she would change sides. The nails on the back feet appeared to be some three-quarters of an inch long and curved slightly downward.

Occasionally she would elevate her rear end by using the tail (bobbed rather short, probably by a predator), and I could see that the hole was at least six or seven inches in diameter. When she probed the bottom with one of her back feet, the trailing edge of her shell would disappear into the hole. I later estimated that those back legs probably were eight or nine inches long and deduced that the hole must have been about that deep, perhaps a little deeper.

When the hole was completed, the turtle raised the back part of her body four or five inches above the opening by pushing up with both rear legs and tucked her stubby tail down into the hole. The egg-laying process was starting.

At first I could only see the small edges of the eggs as they dropped into the hole, but that left no doubt about what she was doing. After each egg fell—or at least after each series of eggs—she would settle onto the hole while using both back legs to position them in the hole.

I moved some twenty-five feet to the right—still hidden by the brush—and from there the binoculars made it seem like I was sitting on the front row. There I learned that the eggs usually came as singles. Now and again there would be two, but I never saw more than two eggs come out at one time.

There was no way to get an accurate count of the eggs, but I estimated that there were somewhere between fifty and seventy-five, each egg being at least three-quarters of an inch in diameter and almost round.

When the eggs were in place, the turtle reached out alternately with her two back legs and started pulling loose earth back into the hole. After pulling in half a cup or so of the loose earth, she would elevate her rear end by using her tail like a jack and hang both feet into the hole to tamp the loose earth down on and around the eggs. During this part of the operation she appeared to make fists of both back feet and use the back surface of the feet for tamping.

Throughout the digging and the refilling of the hole, the turtle rested frequently, appearing to pant and shake with exhaustion. But there were no pauses from the time she started depositing her eggs in the hole until she was finished, except for the time she spent getting the eggs positioned in the hole.

When the loose earth had been pulled back over the eggs she reached far to both sides with both back feet to level off the earth. Then she released some water from her body on the spot.

When it was all over the turtle turned sideways to look over the spot, then ambled toward the water. I stepped out of the brush to get a better picture of the proceedings and she retreated to the water so fast that I thought for a moment she might cartwheel it.

I stood there for several minutes before I could believe what I had seen. Many are called, but few are chosen.

A year or so later my perspective on the turtle kingdom and its relationship to the remainder of the brutal natural world came into even better focus at the edge of my driveway, no more than fifteen or twenty feet from the pond.

We were overrun with raccoons that year because the Scifres family is a soft touch and the word seems to be passed along from one generation to the next. At times we had thirteen to fifteen coons of varying ages on our front sidewalk.

I had not thought for some time about the baby ducks and the smorgasbord they had provided for the turtles in our pond. But as I walked down to the mailbox on an afternoon in late June I noticed a small hole in the earth at the side of the driveway. What was clearly the track of the front foot of a raccoon was in the moist earth that had been removed to create the hole.

At first I could but marvel that a raccoon had dug up a yellowjacket or bumblebee nest to feed on the larvae. Then I noticed a celluloidlike, cream-colored material which appeared to come from some kind of tiny sphere, say half or two-thirds the size of a golfball.

"Well I'll be dogged," I said to my changing world.

A few minutes later I guided my wife and daughters to the spot and pointed out the coon track and the remains of the eggshells while repeating the things I had told them when they were demanding that I get out my squirrel rifle and kill the turtles because they were eating the baby ducks.

"Nature is not always pretty," I said, "but the chickens always seem to come home to roost."

I have not heard any demands since then to kill anything,

and when at midwinter I caution my wife and daughters that there is a daddy longlegs living in the upper corner of the back bathroom shower stall, I can feel assured that he will make it to spring—if not drygulched by a spider.

My association with turtles is a thing of long standing, but during the years when I was growing up at Crothersville it was largely a matter of bringing in meat for the table. Turtles were more or less just one more species of game to be hunted, and they could be taken in any season and in any way.

Undoubtedly the grandest turtle coup I ever participated in came when I was about thirteen years old.

With Dale Isenhower, a boyhood hunting and fishing buddy who still lives in Crothersville, I was fishing a small stream called Buck Creek about half a mile north of town on a hot August day when we noticed a large snapper walking away from the creek bank.

We watched the turtle long enough to see that it was headed for a shallow-water swamp, then tied a strong cord to its tail and tethered it to a sapling.

We figured if this turtle was headed for the swamp there probably would be others there too, so we took off our shoes, rolled up our trouser legs and waded into the swamp, probing the deep muck of the bottom with our toes.

Before long one of us made contact with a snapper's back, but at that point we temporarily ran out of ideas. Neither of us wanted to reach a hand down into the muck to pull out the turtle.

We soon determined that if we each cut a green stick the size of a broom handle we could pry the turtle to the surface. Once there, we could grab it by the tail to avoid its strong and vicious mouth.

In an hour or so we had dug up eighteen turtles. That brought a problem of transportation, until we found a green sapling that had been cut and stripped of its limbs. Each turtle was tied by the tail with lengths of cord, then tied to the sapling. With the sapling resting on our shoulders we could carry the turtles into town without getting bit.

I was leading the way as we walked the Pennsylvania Railroad tracks back to town. Just about the time we reached the city limits I noticed the pole seemed to be making a strange forward-backward motion that it had not been making before.

Once or twice I heard the snap of a turtle's jaws right behind me, but I didn't connect it with a playful effort of my friend Dale to give the foremost and largest turtle a shot at my posterior. When I did connect the two it was too late. The turtle had already made the connection, and for a few minutes we were dancing cheek to cheek. I can assure you there was no romance in the air.

I dropped my end of the pole in sheer fright. Dale dropped his end because he was laughing so hard he couldn't hold it. Fortunately the cloth of my jeans was between my skin and the turtle's strong jaws, and Dale was able to pull the critter off to leave no more than a V-shaped bruise on my posterior.

It took three hours for the two of us to clean the turtles. When we finished we had two of those old stone crocks and a couple of smaller pans of turtle meat.

Dale claimed one crock, I took the other, and we distributed the rest to neighbors.

Cooner

"WE JUST FOUND a baby raccoon down by the pond," the voice on the telephone said. "What should we do with it?"

The voice was that of Nancy, my wife. She was calling me at work late in the afternoon on an early summer day in 1977.

"Leave it right where you found it," I said, dealing out my stock answer for those who call about finding wildlife babies. "Leave it alone and the mother will be back to take care of it."

That didn't work.

"It's just a little thing," Nancy said. "The girls and I were walking down to the pond and could hear it whimpering. Its ears are full of little worms and it's a mess. I think we'd better try to do something for it. I think it needs something to eat."

By now I could see the first question was only a formality. The decision had been made before her call.

"Well," I said, "mix some condensed milk with water and a little Karo syrup and heat it lukewarm. You may be able to get it started eating by dipping your finger in the milk and rubbing it on its lips, or it may take it out of a medicine dropper. If it lives until tomorrow you can take it to the vet."

Well, that baby coon did indeed take the condensed milk-water-Karo mixture from a medicine dropper, and it did live until the next day. As a matter of fact, Cooner, as she became known to our family and friends, lived for some nine years, as near as we can tell.

The next morning Nancy and the girls took baby Cooner, already a family pet, to Dr. Everett Fleming and Dr. James T. Ward at the Allisonville Animal Hospital. When they brought her back home she was the rage of the sage.

She wasn't really old enough yet to play with the girls—Donna, Joan and Patty—but they vied for chances to feed her and do other things that would make her comfortable. I even got into the act.

With the girls helping I used some old lumber to make the frame for a cage some seven feet long, four feet wide and four feet high. It had a solid wood floor and sides of baby chicken wire. Before we finished there was a hollow cardboard den suspended from the top—eventually to be replaced by a real hollow beech limb, because even treated cardboard was not strong enough to hold Cooner.

Cooner grew as fast as the weeds of summer. When it became obvious that she would make it, there were more trips to the vets' office for all kinds of shots, and we soon realized that we would not be far down the road before it would be time to make some decisions about Cooner's future.

Everyone in our family knew the story of Elsa the lion, and we all wanted Cooner to have a shot at life in the wild. We agreed to keep her until she made this decision for herself.

In a few weeks she was eating almost anything we gave her—though she was not fond of raw meat—and liked nothing better than to play with the girls. Late in the summer we started training her for her reentry into the wild by turning her loose to climb the trees and explore the pond. But she always came back to her cage in the garage late in the afternoon, and if she seemed reluctant to return we needed only to peck on the bottom of a pie pan with our knuckles. That would bring her helter-skelter from the top of the big tulip poplar—at times I feared she might fall.

Although Cooner spent most days during the ensuing school year in her garage cage, the return of the girls from school in the afternoon meant the beginning of playtime, and it almost always continued until the adults' bedtime.

Cooner never drew blood, but she would growl at times and bite lightly or kick with those back legs. Still, we could do just about as we pleased with her. My favorite way to play with her was to grasp both front legs with one hand, both back legs with the other, and wear her like a fluffy scarf around the back of my neck. She loved it, and when I would not take the time to hold her in this manner, she would sit on my back behind my head and sift through my hair with her front paws.

When the kids raked leaves, Cooner raked leaves; when the kids rode bikes, Cooner was on their backs with front paws around their necks, and she often got to go to bed with them. They even climbed trees together. Little wonder that she became the star of the show at our house.

I wrote the Department of Natural Resources to get an application for a permit to keep Cooner and filled it out. But each time I started to send it in Cooner appeared to be ready to make the transition back to the wild. So the application remained on my desk through a very mean winter. That was the winter of the blizzard.

There was more than a foot of snow in our side yard for at least six weeks after the heavy snow on the night of January 25, 1978. During that time many wild animals and birds perished for lack of food and because of the extremely cold air temperatures. But Cooner, while getting a little restless, was safe in our garage and house.

I don't remember the date of the big thaw that year, but one Sunday the temperature skyrocketed well above freezing and the little creek behind the house was filled with water.

I was working around the yard most of that afternoon. Cooner followed me around when she wasn't probing holes in the banks and otherwise exploring the creek.

All was going well, but when I tried to lure Cooner back into the garage she wouldn't go. Neither would she be tempted by a pie pan of food, and when I tried to pick her up she resisted violently.

Cooner was more than just ready for a return to the wild. She was also feeling the urge to mate for the first time.

It was a bittersweet night at our house. But this was what we had wanted from the start. Now it had happened.

We saw no more of her for several days. Finally I spotted a raccoon high in a poplar tree in the woodlot behind our stretch of the old Indiana Railway right-of-way and figured it had to be Cooner. When she did not respond to my calls, I banged on the bottom of a pie pan with my knuckles. She ignored me.

Thinking she might be having trouble finding food, I filled a half-gallon milk carton with chunks of raw carrots, apples and cheese and threw in a liberal scoop of dry dog food before tacking the container to the trunk of the poplar tree out of the reach of dogs.

The food was gone the next day and Cooner was still high in the tree, so I filled the container again. This went on for several days, but then Cooner disappeared completely.

For several weeks we saw and heard nothing from Cooner. Secretly we all were upset.

Late one June evening while we were watching television in the living room our little dog, Sugar, went berserk and we found the brick ledge outside the picture window infested with coons.

Cooner, at last, had returned. That little white patch of whiskers in the otherwise black cheek and that big black tip at the end of the tail left no doubt. But there was more. She had brought her three babies for us to see. They were cuter than speckled bird-dog pups.

From that time on the big beech tree, which had been opened up as a coon den when the big leaning tree on the south side of the pond went down, was Cooner's home. We watched her babies grow up, and they in turn became so tame that they would play around the lawn chairs as we relaxed in the front yard in the afternoons.

As a matter of fact, we strongly suspect that we will find Cooner's remains when we have the old tree cut some day to keep it from falling onto other trees. But as this is written a descendant of Cooner lives in the tree and brings her four babies out late in the afternoon for our amusement. There can be little doubt that this sow is of Cooner's lineage—the brown spot between the shoulders on the back, not to mention the mannerisms, being our proof.

After Cooner's successful reentry into the wild she still would come in the house now and then, but she was never at ease there. It seemed she knew she belonged outdoors just as well as we did.

Cooner spent nearly all of each of the nine years of her life in that tree, and she produced young in all but two of them. Each year we would see a lot of Cooner and her young, but at times on hot summer afternoons she would come alone—especially if I were working outside—and would follow me around. Of course, I always stopped what I was doing to get her something to eat, but at times she would snub the food. I had to conclude that our relationship went considerably further than a piece of cheese.

Cooner was always willing to share her tree and home grounds with her young, but in late summer or early fall each year she would disappear with her babies and come back alone two or three weeks later. We always assumed she was taking her young out to find territories of their own, but most of the time they came back, even if it took a while.

Like other raccoons, Cooner more or less hibernated when deep snow and extremely low temperatures hit in winter. When this happened we would implement our big airlift, and the coons that shared the big beech den at that time of year would eat like kings.

I would tape two cane poles together to get added length, tie a cardboard half-gallon milk container to the small end of the makeshift pole and swing the container gently like the pendulum on a clock. When the container disappeared into the hole I would drop the tip of the pole. This would shower the inhabitants with all kinds of goodies, often including pieces of cookies and other preferred items.

One winter late in Cooner's life she disappeared during an extremely cold and snowy period. When she did not respond to the airlift we assumed she was in trouble.

The entire household fretted over Cooner's absence for two or three weeks.

As the coldest day of the year prepared to turn into darkness I went out to open the garage door so Donna could drive in without stopping on the snow-covered driveway when she got home from work.

Soon I heard her car coming up the driveway and the car door slam in the garage. Then Donna burst into the house shouting "Daddy! Daddy! There's a coon in the garage!"

Indeed there was. And it was Cooner. She was skinny as a rail and hungry as a lumberjack. But she was eating high on the hog in a matter of minutes.

I left the garage door cracked as darkness came on and the bottom dropped out of the thermometer. Cooner could have left at any time. But she was still there well after dark, so I closed the door.

I opened the door every day thereafter, but Cooner was no dummy. She slept in a bushel basket of burlap bags next to a heated wall and ate when she felt like it. When the weather broke, she went back to her tree.

One summer night we returned home to find a raccoon that had been hit by a car at the end of our driveway. The head was damaged so badly that I could not find the little cluster of white hairs in the black spot of the cheek, but I was sure it was Cooner.

I gathered up the body with the idea of giving Cooner a decent burial the next morning. By bedtime I—like all the other members of the family—was a wreck. At 2:00 A.M. I had not been able to sleep, so I went to the kitchen, poured myself a stiff bit of brandy (which I seldom touch) and sat in the dark of the living room, sipping and thinking things over.

I must have been there half an hour or more when something told me to turn on the porch light.

When I flipped the switch, I saw an old sow coon standing

on her back legs looking up at the door glass, probably wondering whether she would get her supper.

I couldn't believe it, but there it was—the little clump of white hairs in the black cheek patch.

My world had taken a change for the better.

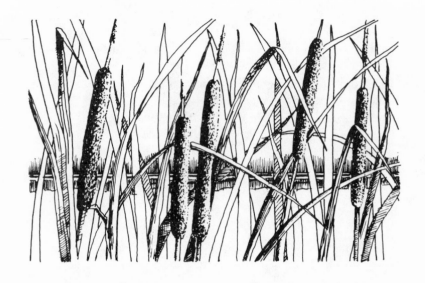

Never Trust a Cattail

WHEN WE BOUGHT the property on 111th Street the pond was lined with large clumps of yellow and purple iris. It was a beautiful thing to see toward the end of May when they bloomed.

Unfortunately—or fortunately, if one has any preservationist blood in one's veins, which I do—the pond also hosted muskrats in fair numbers.

In the spring we would marvel at the beauty of the iris and a month or so later we would watch the little muskrats out for tours of the pond late in the afternoon with their mothers. But, alas, clumps of yellow and purple iris are not compatible with mama and papa muskrats, who combine their talents to turn out young in sizable numbers.

And so it was—since yellow and purple iris roots provided the only ready supply of food on our pond—that as the muskrat population grew the iris population dwindled.

Eventually we learned the saddest lesson of all: that while it may be nice to leave nature alone to do its thing (as the true preservationists are wont to do), the results can be—and often are—something less than desirable for humans. Eventually the beautiful irises were no more because the muskrats were.

Realizing the plight of the iris was bad enough, but we rationalized it away by telling ourselves that since the pond no longer provided an abundance of food, the muskrat population also would fade somewhat. We were more right than we cared to be.

Not only did the muskrat population fade somewhat, it disappeared completely, just as the iris had gone. The muskrats were not eaten, however; they left of their own free will, apparently seeking other ponds with other clumps of iris. We were stuck with barren pond banks.

"They'll come back," I told Nancy when she fretted over the absence of the pretty iris the following spring, but as that summer and the next passed without their return it became more and more evident that the muskrats had cleaned out the roots.

That set my mind to working overtime. We needed some kind of vegetation around the edge of the pond, and one day while I was fishing in the southern part of the state the thought hit me that cattails might be the answer. It would, at least, be worth a try.

On my next trip south I took along my garden spade and dug up three cattail plants from a patch I had selected with some care. Admittedly, I did not know what physical characteristics one should look for in selecting a desirable strain of cattail. Not knowing at the time that I would have had to mulch them and burn the mulch to do them in, I wrapped the roots—huge balls of mud—of each plant in damp burlap for the trip to their new home.

It was much too late to plant them when I arrived home that night, but the next morning I surveyed the pond carefully and finally decided that the cattails should be planted at the north end, in the edge of the shallow water.

Nothing much happened with the cattails that year, except that I spent quite a lot of time admiring them—and the green thumb I had displayed in transplanting them with such success.

Early the next summer I noticed I had six cattail plants in the cluster. The year after that there were thirteen. Then they went berserk, with plants showing up even at the far end of the pond, a good forty yards away from the original planting.

The following summer I counted twenty-seven in one area at the north end of the pond. With that I started talking with my old friend Will E. (Bill) Madden, because he had fought cattails for many years at Willow Slough State Fish and Wildlife Area and I figured he knew of which he spoke.

"The only way to control cattails, short of pulling them up by the roots," he said, "is with chemicals."

Of course, chemicals could not be used on my pond.

I later learned that cattails can be killed by covering them with wide strips of black plastic, which cut off the life-giving rays of the sun while generating intense heat. But that would have been far too slow. Bill Madden was right. The only real and immediate way to deal with cattails is to pull them up by the roots. Solving the cattail problem, wherever it may be, is that back-breaking simple.

My first attempts at ridding the pond of at least some of the cattails, which by now were threatening to take the north end of the pond and had gained a solid foothold in the south, were pinned on the hope that I could dig them out with a garden spade.

Indeed, I could. But jamming the spade down on all

sides of each cattail plant before lifting it out of the water and muck took a lot of time. Furthermore, I soon saw that while I might win the battle in this manner, I probably would lose the war. I was merely cutting the roots the plant was sending out in the mucky bottom of the pond to start new cattails, and these starts would undoubtedly be successful.

No! There was only one way to pull cattail roots, and that was to get in there with them, work my fingers and hands under the main root system of the plant and pull it straight up with gut-wrenching effort.

In pulling cattails up by the roots, one of the first things I noticed was a very white root, which had a smooth surface and looked very much like a marlin spike. This root told the whole story of how the cattail increases its numbers. No need to read it in a book; it was all right there before my eyes.

As I already suggested, the plant merely sends this spikelike root out through the mud bottom of the pond, or even the earth. When it is out there some fourteen to eighteen inches, the spike puts down roots of its own and sprouts a new plant. The new plant will, in turn, send out spikes, possibly the same year. Eventually several plants may be connected in a common system, but any one of the plants can grow independently of the others and any one can send out spikes in other directions. That is why an assault on a single cattail with chemicals can influence plants several feet away.

I had known of cattail roots being used as food around Crothersville when I was a kid, but I don't think our family tried them more than once or twice. Still, when I started seeing those pure white shoots, the thought of another culinary caper came to the fore.

The books of many experts on natural foods had suggested the roots of the cattail can be delightful table fare, but none ever seemed to get real specific on the matter. The roots I had seen prior to my discovery of the white spikes did not even look appetizing.

I started slicing rings off one of the spikes (they were very much like carrot rings) and noticed that at about the point where the spike turned greenish the texture of the root became pithy, much like a radish. But even at that there appeared to be much edible about the spikes and I started saving them as I pulled up the plants. (Incidentally, if a white spike breaks off and is free in water, it will float.)

By the time my first cattail-pulling session ended I had a whole saucepan's worth of white spikes strewn about the grassy shore of the pond.

I didn't have time to cook them that evening, but I did clean them up with cold tap water at the kitchen sink and the next day embarked upon a cattail-root eating spree, the mere thought of which still taunts my taste buds.

That first batch was stewed with just enough water to cover them and a little piece of bacon. I had, of course, sampled them raw the night before when I was cleaning them up and had concluded that they would not detract a whit from the taste of a fresh green salad.

From there I tried frying them like potatoes—a little onion and chopped bacon added—but the real culinary caper came when I parboiled them with onion and bacon, then simmered them slowly in a cream sauce made with milk from a margarine-flour base. Actually, what we are talking about is a thin gravy. Since that time I have not found anything that you can add to the cattail roots and onion that will wreck the dish, including fresh, dried or frozen morel mushrooms or any one of several other edible fungi, fresh or frozen peas, whole kernel corn and who knows what else. When I get started cooking, as you may have sensed by now, I usually have some fun.

Incidentally, if the sauce gets thick enough to support sliced boiled eggs and little chunks of American cheese—even something with a stronger cheese flavor, if you like—the dish can be given still another dimension. The sauce pan should be covered to melt the cheese in the mild heat.

There were, of course, reasons other than the fact that they provided some pretty good country table fare for having cattails on the pond.

Wood ducks, mallards and a smattering of other winged critters found sanctuary among the cattails from would-be enemies, and one of the most pleasant of all activities came in the nesting of the red-winged blackbird. Although the return of the wood duck has always signaled the arrival of spring for me, the return of this blackbird and its selection of a nesting site in the old growth of the cattails is something special at our house.

When Clee returns—that is my name for the male red-wing because that seems to be the gist of his song—I start looking for his mate (the two look nothing at all alike). Before long they will be fashioning their nest in the reeds of old cattail growth, dead grasses and other materials a foot or so above the water. While the nest may be in some pretty thick old growth stuff, it will not be far from an opening in the cattails.

Although the handsome Clee may be out gallivanting around with another fair lady, the female guards her nest with such fervor that I often go to the park bench late in the afternoon to sit and watch as other species of birds come there for various reasons. The hen (a handsome bird in her own right—often mistaken for various thrushes because of her brown-streaked breast) takes a high perch from which she can see her nest. When other birds start getting close to the pond she puts them to flight and follows in a menacing manner until they are no longer a threat. Not even the cardinals, which I am certain would not harm her nest or her young, are permitted to roost in the bushes nearby.

The mortality rate of red-wing fledglings must be very high because I seldom see the female attending more than one young bird after the young leave the nest, even though the female usually sits three or four eggs. Even at that the female red-wing is a dutiful and doting mother who devotes her life to feeding her young.

I once watched and shot pictures with a telephoto lens while a mother red-wing brought in what appeared to be winged insects to a fledgling sitting on a cattail stalk. Each time she brought in an insect I would shoot a picture and this went on for no more than ten minutes. When my film was processed I could see that the female had made at least six trips to the young bird in that short time, each time with an insect. During that time, the female also had spent some time shielding the young bird from the sun by sitting directly above it and spreading her wings.

It could also be that my strong attraction to cattails transcends both my taste buds and my love of Mother Nature's children. It could be that when I am out there pulling cattails, I am actually on an ego trip . . . sort of giving my male chauvinistic tendencies a chance to strut their stuff.

You see, for nearly four decades I have lived in a world of females. The only other male on the property is a long-haired old yellow cat I know as Mr. Fizzwater, and he does not carry his sword at a jaunty angle anymore.

Mr. Fizzwater had trouble with his urinary tract soon after arriving as a stray at my little world some ten or twelve years ago. All of his piping had to be replaced with plastic tubing (at a cost of well over $100). He now is healthy as the proverbial little fat pig while eating $24-per-case cat food; as round as a basketball, and as loving as a cat can be. Mr. Fizzwater pays his freight by being the only other quasi-male on the property.

If I might philosophize a bit right here, I would interject the observation that even though man may gain "dominion over the fish of the sea, and over the fowl of the air, and over every thing that moveth upon the earth" (Genesis 1:28), in a world of females he is just another critter.

Ivan Sipes, one of the old codgers I used to listen to at night on the liars' bench outside Applegate's Grocery Store at Crothersville, more or less put it in perspective when he said: "You got to watch these guys who tell you they rule the roost at home because they'll lie to you about other things, too."

Thus, I do not doubt for a moment that the quality of my cattail-pulling experiences over the years has been enhanced by the fact that all of my daughters and some of their friends have helped. Preteen girls tend to outgrow this notion that being caked with mud from head to toe can be fun, but it was good while it lasted.

With these young females giving me the opportunity to decide on such issues as "Where should we put them, Dad?" or "Should we pull the dead ones, too?" and other dire matters, I got a rare feeling of importance.

In short, if Ivan ever had seen me pulling cattails with my daughters, he undoubtedly would have bestowed upon me the title of "high muckety-muck."

Santa Was a Mink

"I DON'T LIKE IT any better than you do," my mother, Laura Bell Scifres, said in a conversation with my father in the kitchen. "But the kids will just have to want this year. We'll have a good Christmas dinner with some candy and fruit and use the money we would have spent on Christmas for the bills."

I was barely old enough to know the truth about Santa—or wouldn't admit it, at least. But when I heard my mother say that, the "genuine pigskin" football I wanted for Christmas seemed very distant. For weeks I had looked at the picture of the football in the mail-order catalog and dreamed of having it. Now I knew it would not happen.

Suddenly this was something I wanted to tell someone, but I knew this couldn't happen, either. Not my older brother or sister, not my grandma, not anyone. I wasn't eaves-dropping—simply taking a nap on a mid-December Saturday morning on the old black-leather davenport in the living room—when my mother made the statement that clanged in my ears like a giant hammer on an anvil.

My mother wasn't angry with anyone; she was merely stating the economic facts of our family life as she talked with my father in the kitchen.

It didn't mean anything to me at the time, but the nation was just beginning to escape the stranglehold of the Depression years. I did know times were hard because my mother had to work at the shoe factory when work was available. Through it all my dad had managed to find some work, too, and we had been luckier than many families. But now the grocer, while very patient, was pressing more for payment of back bills, my mother said, and the coal man and other merchants were becoming reluctant to extend more credit.

Everything was quiet for a short time when my mother stopped talking. Then my dad said he had some things to do in the woodshed.

I continued to feign my nap for several minutes after the back door opened and closed. Then I remembered seeing the stub of a rope tied to a rafter in the woodshed of an abandoned house on the other side of town, and that brought frightful memories of the stories about how a man had hanged himself there two years before because he could not provide food for his family. I got up from the couch quietly, pulled on the old hand-me-down sheepskin coat I had been using as a blanket, and slipped quietly out the front door.

There were no sounds as I neared the woodshed, and the worst possible fears raced through my mind. For a time I hesitated, not knowing whether to open the door. But on opening the door I was much relieved to find my father bending over the large wooden chest which contained his tools.

Spread out on top of the tool chest were several rusty steel traps and the parts of many others. He was looking at each trap and each piece carefully, placing the best whole traps off to one side and picking out the best parts of the others.

Several years earlier—before I was old enough to remember—the old woodshed had burned to the ground and most of my dad's traps had been destroyed along with his fishing tackle. He loved to hunt, fish and trap, but there was no money to buy new traps or fishing tackle. About the only outdoor pleasure he had left was some hunting, and he did this to provide food for our family.

Once, though, there had been more than a hundred of the steel traps, and during the trapping season each year they had stretched up and down the two forks of the Muscatatuck River, which surrounded our little town of Crothersville, Indiana, and along a number of its smaller tributaries. But the traps had not been touched since my dad sifted through the ruins of the fire and placed them in a nail keg, which had been stored under the house until the new woodshed was completed.

I did not say anything but watched as my dad placed three whole traps off to one side, muttering—as much to himself as to me—that they would still hold a mink. By crimping the broken chains together with baling wire and substituting parts of others, he fashioned five other traps.

"Eight traps," my dad said, now clearly addressing his remarks to me. "That ought to be enough to catch a mink."

Explaining that I was old enough to learn something about mink trapping, my dad said we would go out to set the traps the next day after church. Then he swept the remaining traps and parts back into the nail keg and returned it to its place in the dark corner behind the woodshed door.

I didn't dally along the street with the other children after Sunday school the next day but went straight home.

When the family had finished dinner (dinner was the noon meal and supper the evening meal in those days), my dad pulled on his hip boots and we left town walking northward on the Pennsylvania Railroad tracks. Skipping one crosstie with each stride was just a normal step for my dad, a tall, thin man, but my legs were not long enough for that. I had to step on every crosstie, and I almost had to move at a run to keep up.

My dad carried no gun—hunting on Sunday was both immoral and unlawful in those days. But the traps made a musical jangling sound in the game pouch of his hunting coat, and many of my thoughts were of Christmas.

The town was long out of sight before we found the first good mink sign at a place where the water of a small stream had washed the earth away from the roots of a large maple tree, leaving a protected undercut ledge at the edge of the water.

"Look," my dad said, standing knee-deep in the creek, "he comes down over the bank right there and walks along the edge of the water." His hand swept slowly along the ledge, showing me the mink tracks in the soft mud covered by an inch or so of water.

My dad took two of the traps from his hunting coat and tested them to make sure they were in good working order. Then he placed them in the shallow water at the spot where the mink stepped over a small black root as it left the earth ledge and went into deeper water.

He covered the traps carefully with wisps of wet, dead grass and leaves taken from the bottom of the stream after they had been staked securely with a strong ash fork cut from the top of a sapling far back in a nearby thicket.

"Never cut a trap stake close to the place you will set traps," he said as he cut the stake. "That tells the world there are traps nearby, and you may come back to find your traps gone."

Continuing my first lesson in mink trapping as we walked away from the set, my dad said that if you find a place where a mink has been, the chances are good you can catch it.

"A mink will always come back," he said, "if he don't get caught somewhere else."

We found several other places where mink had been as the afternoon wore on, and one was a beautiful series of holes in the bank of a small stream. There were holes both above and below the water line around the roots of a willow tree and mink dung on a partly inundated piece of driftwood nearby. But my dad made no move to set traps there. He would not even go near the place because he said it was a den.

"You don't fool around a mink's den if you want to trap him," he said. "If you do, he may hightail it right out of the country."

We made three other sets during the afternoon—two traps at each place—and each time my dad explained why he positioned the traps as he did and what he expected the mink to do that would cause it to step in the traps.

At each set he pushed a strong stick into the bottom of the creek a foot or so toward deep water from the point where the traps rested, and at the third set my curiosity had to be satisfied. I asked about the stick.

He explained that in each case the stick was an obstruction placed so the trap chain would wrap around it and keep a trapped animal from getting to the bank. It was meant to hasten drowning.

"A mink is a wily water devil," my dad said, adding that when a mink is trapped or otherwise in trouble, the first thing it will do is get in water if it can.

Just before dark we placed the last two traps in a little dishpan-sized hole of water three or four inches deep at a point where a tile drain came out of the high bank of the stream. From the little pool the water drained eight or ten feet through a shallow, ditchlike depression and into the stream.

"We'll catch that big fellow," my dad said, almost in a whisper, as he pointed to several places where the mink had left tracks in the mud as it followed the trickle of water to the tile opening. "This is an awful good place."

With the last of the eight traps set, we headed for home, stopping occasionally as my dad pointed out a squirrel scurrying out of a corn stubble field to a den in the woods, an owl coming out of its den in a big hollow sycamore tree, and a number of other birds and animals either settling on roosts or coming out for the night.

It was well after dark when we got home and the rest of the family had eaten a supper of leftovers from the noon meal.

We ate alone in the kitchen, and as my dad sipped his coffee he explained that we would not run the traps before the middle of the week. This would give the elements a chance to wash away the scent we had left at the four sets.

Each night after supper we would sit around the old Parlour Furnace in the big room that served as living quarters for the family during the winter months, and invariably the talk would evolve to the fact that there could be a big mink stepping in one of our traps at that very moment. Other members of the family were not so optimistic, but I believed it and I am sure my dad did.

Each day I would run home from school in the afternoon with the hope that we might run the traps. A few extra days of work had come, however, and my dad could not turn down a chance to earn some money.

After supper on Wednesday evening my dad said we would run the traps. He brought the rusty old kerosene lantern in from the woodshed, washed the globe in the dishpan with warm water, shined it with a sheet of newspaper, then filled the lantern with kerosene before we went off into the night.

At the first set some of the leaves and grass had drifted away from the traps, and my dad repaired the set. While doing so he pointed out that once you get traps set you shouldn't get any closer to them than you have to.

"Leave them alone," he said, explaining that if the traps are uncovered you must repair the set. But otherwise, you should check the traps from a good distance.

At the last set—the two traps at the entrance to the tile drain—my dad left me standing at the edge of the creek's brushy banks and waded across to check the traps alone.

"I'll come back and get you if we have a mink," he said, obviously sensing my disappointment at not being able to participate. "I don't want to disturb this place any more than necessary."

When the dim light of the lantern had disappeared below the high bank of the creek, I stood quietly in the dark. The sounds of my dad pushing through the brush and wading the creek were reassuring, but I imagined all kinds of things could happen to me alone there.

Far to the north hounds bawled mournfully, and once I heard the beat of massive wings very close. Soon, though, a faint shaft of light showed momentarily over the banks of the creek and then the lantern popped up. It was a welcome sight.

"Nothing there either," my dad said, cocking his head to the north and adding in the same breath: "Somebody's having a good coon chase."

As we headed across a field to hit the first of several rough trails we would follow, my dad said we'd better hurry. "We could get wet before we get home," he said, motioning to dark cloud banks scudding in low from the southwest.

Before we reached the first dim street light at the edge

of town a misty rain was falling. It seemed to make my dad happy.

"This could be the night we'll get him," he told me. "Everything will run tonight . . . if it just don't freeze."

I went straight to bed because I had to go to school the next morning. But I lay awake for some time thinking about the events of the night, and before drifting off to sleep the patter on the roof told me the rain was coming down harder.

Everyone else had gone to bed—my grandmother always said we went to bed with the chickens (meaning very early). But my dad sat in the dark by the living room window for an hour or more with a cup of warmed-up coffee and watched the rain turn to a wet snow as the big flakes fell past the street light across the street.

The snow—more dry and sticking on the earth by morning—continued through the day, and just before dusk the bottom seemed to drop out of the thermometer on our sheltered front porch.

At bedtime that night when my dad banked the living room stove with large chunks of coal brought in from the front porch, he said the temperature was close to zero.

"That will ruin our chances," he told me. "Our traps probably are already frozen up, except for the two at the tile drain."

He explained that the little pool of water at the tile drain would remain free of ice longer than the creek because the water coming out of the tile was much warmer than creek water. But he said if the cold weather continued, even this water would freeze because the runoff from the fields would stop. Then, he said, even those traps would freeze.

The cold wave had not broken when I got up to go to school the next morning—the last day of school before Christmas vacation. As I had breakfast at the big table in the kitchen, my dad was getting ready to go to work.

"If we don't have a mink now," he said, "we won't catch one."

Then, as if trying to let my hopes down a little easier, he explained that we could try again after Christmas—or even before—if a thaw came.

"We'll run our traps and take them up tomorrow," he said.

When we left the town just before noon on Saturday my dad cradled his old sixteen-gauge Model 97 Winchester pump gun in the crook of his left arm, saying that we would do some rabbit tracking between sets and that with a little luck we would have fried rabbit for dinner on Sunday.

Both traps at the first set had been thrown before they were frozen in the shallow water of the stream, and this made me optimistic. But my dad explained that the traps probably had been thrown by the current of the stream, not by a mink.

The traps at the next two sets also were frozen solid in the ice of the little creek. My dad chopped them free with his hatchet and placed them in the back of his hunting coat with the others.

It was more than a mile to the last set. To get there we went through a big thicket and several weed patches. At the thicket my dad said we would try some rabbit hunting.

When we found the first rabbit tracks in the snow, my dad showed me how to follow the tracks, emphasizing that the hunter should always keep his eyes on the tracks well ahead.

Twice we followed rabbit tracks into the jumbled thicket, but the tracks crossed and crisscrossed the tracks of other rabbits and were lost. When our tracking efforts did not produce rabbits, my dad forced his way into the heavy cover of blackberry canes and other brush and soon had jumped several, one running nearly between my legs.

In the next hour my dad bagged three rabbits without missing a shot.

It was late afternoon by the time we reached the last two traps at the tile drain. My dad told me to stand at the edge of the bank as I had the night we ran the traps.

I did not protest, but my dad must have noticed my disappointment and told me to come along. We would take up the last two traps together.

After my dad slid down the steep bank and was standing on the ice of the creek, he motioned for me to do likewise. Then, crossing the creek on the ice and walking to the snow-covered tile drain, we were at the end of our miniature trap line.

"The end of Christmas, too," I thought, because even though the traps were covered by snow, there obviously was not a mink there.

I could see the disappointment in my dad's face, but that turned to disbelief when he brushed the snow away to find only one of our two traps.

He wasn't puzzled long. With his gloves off now, he brushed the snow away from the side of the little depression where we had set the traps. He pointed to scratch marks in the earth, and his eyes flashed with anger.

"We had him," he said with trembling voice while crouching dejectedly in the snow with the end of the broken trap chain in his hand. "Somebody beat us here."

Other than our own, there were no tracks in the snow. My dad said this probably meant the mink had been trapped and stolen before the snow ended at dusk the day after we visited the traps at night.

For what seemed like several minutes my dad squatted there with the broken trap chain in his hand and said nothing. Then he stood up and tried to pull up the remaining trap by tugging against the stake with the chain.

The earth was frozen solid, however, and the trap stake would not budge. As he pulled harder the rusty chain parted and he lost his balance, nearly falling in the snow.

That aggravated my dad even more, but as he mumbled more harsh words about trap thieves he stopped abruptly and turned to look at the creek. Then, dropping the trap with the broken chain in the trampled show, he walked to the creek and stooped to scrape snow away from the ice in an area more than a yard square. He dropped to his hands and knees and tried to look down through the ice.

With hands blue from exposure to snow water and cold air, my dad stood up and took his hatchet from the back of his hunting coat. He chopped a hole in the ice almost a foot in diameter and splashed out the ice chips with his hands. Then he removed the hunting coat and his old gray sweater and rolled his left shirtsleeve as high as he could get it before plunging his hand to the bottom of the creek.

For a moment I thought my dad must have lost his mind as his arm swept circles in the ice hole. But before I had time for further speculation he pulled his arm out of the icy water with the missing trap, which held the biggest, blackest mink I had ever seen.

I don't remember much about what happened in the next few minutes. I was much too excited. My dad let me hold the trap and the mink while he rolled down his shirtsleeve and put on his sweater and hunting coat.

As we prepared for the walk home my dad explained that the mink undoubtedly had been trapped the same night we ran the traps and had fought so hard that the rust-weakened chain had broken.

He said he was so sure the trap and mink had been stolen that he had almost forgotten the thing he had tried to impress upon me—that a mink will go to water, if it can get there, any time it is in trouble.

But when he tried to pull up the remaining trap and the chain broke, he realized the mink could have twisted the other chain apart, too. He knew the mink would go to the creek if this were the case.

He said that he could not see the bottom of the creek because the water was still a little murky from the rain but that he knew if the mink was tired from fighting the trap it couldn't swim far with the trap on its leg. His guess was right.

"Looks like we're going to get more snow," my dad said, pointing to the clouds rolling in from the southwest. "We'd better get home."

When we topped the last hill, the lights of the town twinkled in the distance and a gentle snow was falling. As we crossed the last wheat-stubble field and ducked under the single strand of barbed wire which seemed to constitute the town limits, the sounds of the community settling down for another winter night were audible. Here a door slammed and there a dog barked, but the sound I liked best was the tinkle of empty glass milk bottles rattling around in the wire containers as Calvin Groves's milk delivery truck struggled over the snow-filled street to complete the evening delivery.

As we approached the first street light of the town, a group of young carolers huddled on the lawn of a dim-lit house and the words of their carol seemed to mingle and merge with the other sounds.

"Silent night . . . Holy night . . . All is calm . . . All is bright. . . ." I couldn't always hear the words because of the wind, but I knew the song and recited it silently while watching the flickering candles held by the carolers.

I also knew the carolers were singing at this particular house several days before Christmas because the elderly lady who lived there had been in bad health for some time and there was talk around town that she probably would not live until Christmas.

Remembering the death of a little dog our family had

owned, I knew that death was a sad occasion and did not want to seem disrespectful. But as we approached the first street light I could no longer hold the question which had been running through my mind all the way to town.

"Do you think Santa will come now?" I asked, skipping backward in front of my dad as we passed through the swath of light which came down from the street light above.

My dad turned his head as if he were looking back at the carolers, but not before I noticed moisture on his cheeks. He did not answer my question immediately. But he looked back at me when we were in the darkness again.

I will never lose the picture of my dad at that moment—the old shotgun cradled in the crook of his left arm and his bare right hand resting on the mink in his hunting coat pocket, just as it had been almost constantly from the time we had started home.

Nor will I ever forget his answer to my question.

"He's done been here, Bill," my father said.

Santa did, indeed, come to our house that year. I received a "genuine pigskin" football—even though there could not have been enough time for my parents to order it from the mail-order catalog.

The rubber bladder was splotched with many patches and the seams of the cover were parting at several places before my football finally gave up the ghost.

Moreover, the thaw my dad had spoken of did come just after Christmas and we did, indeed, put the traps out again. Before the trapping season ended we would catch three other mink—none so exciting as the first—and many of our family's bills would be paid.

It took many years to soak in, but eventually I realized that my parents gave me much more than a football for Christmas that year—they gave me a way of life.

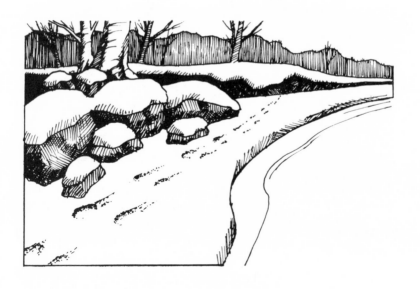

Christmas Vacation

THE COMMERCIALIZATION of Christmas was getting up a pretty good head of steam when I was an early teener in the late 1930s at Crothersville, but one of the finest gifts boys and girls received was the week or more when the school was closed.

It was a time for rabbit hunting, mink tracking, sledding on Heller's Hill or ice skating on small lakes and ponds or even the grand old Muscatatuck River if the weather had been cold enough and there was no snow to cover the ice.

Snow or no, we could always depend on a lot of outdoor activities, and when we descended on Snow's Restaurant late at night for gigantic cheeseburgers with cottage fries and hot chocolate there never was a thought that life could ever be any better.

So it was on a blustery, snow-filled Friday night in 1940 when our Christmas vacation had just begun.

Fine, dry snow had started swirling down just before darkness came, but it was too late to cancel the high school basketball game. The opposition was undoubtedly already halfway there. So the game went on, and when it was over half the town had gathered at the restaurant for the postmortem.

I was sitting at the soda counter sipping a cherry Coke (the tab for a fountain Coke was a nickel, incidentally) when Jack Cain, one of several of my older outdoor (hunting and fishing) mentors, headed for home.

"If it quits snowing before daylight, tomorrow is going to be a good day to track a mink," Jack said, pausing behind me. "If you want to go, be at my house just before daylight."

Then he was gone.

I did want to go, and I was at Jack's house the next morning before daylight with my little single-shot Springfield rifle. Before the first streaks of gray started showing in the east we were mushing through six inches of fresh, dry snow as we headed for the Muscatatuck River bottoms some two miles to the east.

The street lights were burning brightly and the temperature hovered at four below zero when we left town that morning. The street lights were burning when we returned, too, and while temperatures did rise some during the afternoon, the thermometer at Jack's house stood on zero when we returned.

The time between was the thing—or things—of which stories are made.

As we plowed our way across corn and wheat stubble fields, through thickets and woods, Jack explained that conditions for tracking a mink were ideal on this morning because the snow had fallen until only a few hours before daylight.

"Most of the tracks will be covered," he said. "If we find mink tracks today we should be able to trail him to a den."

With the fresh new snow on the ground, even the birds were making themselves scarce on this morning. But just before we dropped over the last hill into the floodplain of the river we found where a very large opossum had emerged from a brush pile half the size of an automobile, then had decided to return to his lair.

He was our first victim.

Although we had been walking rather briskly most of the way, the work entailed in uncovering the opossum was welcome. It warmed us up from head to toe and provided the first excitement of the day when Jack reached into the "nest" of leaves and small sticks to bring the big boar out by the tail.

Not wishing to carry a possum half the size of a pig around all day, we stashed our first game near the river bridge half a mile downstream because we knew the weather had not been cold enough to make ice on the river safe for crossing. We would have to cross the river at the Slate Ford Bridge to get into the river bottoms. We also would have to come back that way.

Late in the morning we found the tracks of a mink skirting the edge of the river, but the tracks were difficult to follow because the animal was spending almost as much time in the water as on land. But after a mile or so the mink crossed a large picked cornfield and headed east toward Alf's Bayou.

"That's where we'll catch up with this big boy," Jack said, but the mink followed the bayou banks for about a quarter of a mile, then crossed on the ice.

We couldn't take a chance on the ice—getting wet out there would have meant real trouble—so we circled the bayou and picked up the tracks on the far side.

We followed the mink for nearly a mile in a southwesterly

direction and toward midafternoon (nearly six hours after we first hit the tracks) found where the mink had gone into a hole in the ground on a little mound in the middle of a thicket. White Oak ditch was less than fifty yards away, and there were sheets of ice an inch thick in all of the low places where backwater had stood a week or so earlier and had frozen before the water receded.

Jack whispered that it was not the best place in the world to get a shot at a mink if he came out of there under a full head of steam. But when we circled the spot and found no tracks leaving we knew this was where it would happen, if it did happen.

There were three holes in the mound of earth. Jack stationed me where I could see all three without moving my head before he handed me the old twelve-gauge double barrel he called "Old Hannah" after cautioning me that "both ears (hammers) are back and she's ready to go."

The gun, which sported Damascus wire-twist barrels and fancy hammers, had belonged to Jack's father and undoubtedly had brought down a boxcarload of game in its time.

"Be quiet," Jack said, "and keep your eyes open while I stop up one of the holes. Then we'll see what happens."

Jack stacked strong, short sticks in one of the holes until it was impossible for any animal to get in or out, then took off his hunting coat and stuffed it into the entrance in front of the sticks.

Then he picked up a long, greencut pole he had cut earlier and handed it to me as he reclaimed Old Hannah.

"I'll watch that hole," he said, poking the business end of Old Hannah's barrels at one of the remaining open holes. "When I'm ready you poke the stick in the other hole and make it sound like something is coming in there."

With that Jack took a solid shooting stance over the hole he expected the mink to come out of, recocked both barrels of the shotgun and put it to his shoulder as if he would be shooting at any second. He was all business.

I must confess that I questioned our chances of success as I watched Jack staring down the barrel of Old Hannah in anticipation of the action he thought might come. My doubts grew when no action came in the first minute or so.

But when I slacked the pace with which I pushed the pole into the hole in the earth, Jack urged me on without making a sound.

Seconds later Old Hannah exploded. Jack reached into the hole to bring out a mink—minus the tip of its nose.

"He would have been gone if he ever got out of there and under the ice," Jack said. "I just shot the tip of his nose off."

Jack later explained that a mink is a nervous critter, so he knew when we were sure the mink was there that we probably would get some action.

It was just a matter of making the mink come out of the right hole, he said.

As we celebrated our success Jack told me about a similar experience he and his brother, Alton, had in similar circumstances not far from the spot where we stood.

There were sheets of snow-covered ice almost everywhere, and that time the mink got out of the hole and headed for the sheet ice when Alton fired the same old shotgun and brought down their quarry.

Jack said he asked Alton how in the world he ever hit the mink as it headed for the ice and got a prompt reply: "I saw a twenty-dollar bill on his tail!"

At one point during the day Jack and I were about six miles from home. As we headed in at dusk I went through the skim ice covering a sinkhole and landed on my back some four or five feet below.

Jack pulled me out and brushed away the snow, though, and we made it back to town in spite of my aching back and tired legs.

It was well after dark when I got home that night, but my mother had kept my supper warm in the oven of the old wood stove in the kitchen. By nine o'clock I had rested for a spell and was headed downtown to meet Jack. Together we would sell our fur.

We found the fur buyer—a grand old man named Berb Garriott—at the poolroom. Berb docked us a little because the tip of the mink's nose was gone, but our unskinned catch for the day brought twenty-two dollars and some odd change. My share was a little more than eleven dollars, more than my dad had made that week.

By 10:30 that night I had disappeared in the old feather-bed in my cold room and was covered with piles of home-made quilts. I thought a lot about the events of the day as I drifted off to sleep, but falling in the sinkhole and the pain in my back never crossed my mind.

By midafternoon the next day the money was burning a hole in my pocket. I wanted to buy something so badly that I could almost taste it. But when my mother and I were alone in the kitchen I offered her the money, a ten-dollar bill and a one-dollar bill neatly wrapped around the change.

"No!" she said. "You worked hard for that money—it's yours."

When Squirrels Cut Hickory:
The Story in a Nutshell

I KNOW IT SOUNDS CRAZY to even hint that nutshells might be able to speak. They certainly cannot. Still, these leftovers from a squirrels' smorgasbord constantly tell me stories about the diners and help me immeasurably with my hunts.

Take the hunt I had one Saturday morning many years ago with my father in the Muscatatuck River bottoms west of Uniontown in Jackson County.

We rode the interurban—an electricity-powered rail car—that morning just before daylight from Crothersville north to Langdon Crossing, some four miles from our home.

We entered the east edge of a large woods in the river bottoms about the time the sun came up, then went different directions to cover a greater part of the woods. Squirrels were cutting (feeding) heavily on hickory.

I can't remember how many squirrels we each had the next time I saw my dad some two hours later or the number of squirrels we bagged that day. But when we saw each other we were some sixty yards apart, both headed for—and watching—the same hickory tree. This hickory towered above all the other trees in this part of the woods.

My dad was a little closer to the tree than I was, so when our eyes met I pointed skyward with my hand and index finger to ask if there was a squirrel on the hickory. He spread his hands palms up to let me know he did not know—or at least that he could not say for certain that there was a squirrel on the tree. We did not want to use any audible form of communicating because that would have spooked the squirrel if there had been one on the tree.

Slowly—a step at a time—we closed in on the tree. When we met it was obvious that squirrels were there and were feeding heavily on this tree. The green outer husks and the pieces of hard inner shells littering the forest floor left no doubt about that.

My dad leaned over, picked up a piece of husk and held it out where I could see it. He squeezed the fresh, whitish piece of the husk (we called them cuttings; some pronounced it cut'ins) and moisture oozed out.

"He's up there," he whispered. "Let's just wait him out."

We obviously had interrupted the squirrel's breakfast. It had either seen or heard one of us (probably me) moving toward the tree and had simply quit cutting the nut it was working on.

When a squirrel eats a hickory nut it bites away chunks of the green outer husk until it can get to the hard inner shell. Then with its two long and sharp front teeth it chisels its way through the shell, which gets even harder as the nut matures. It then uses those same two teeth, which drop out of the foremost point of the upper jaw, to extract the nut kernels or pieces thereof.

I speak with authority when I say one cannot realize how long and how sharp those two front teeth are until one has been bitten by a squirrel.

Quietly, I moved fifteen or twenty yards to the north to get a better view of the uppermost part of the big hickory.

My dad stood motionless in his tracks.

For what seemed a very long time—probably ten or fifteen minutes—neither of us moved. Eventually the quiet paid off.

A piece of outer husk dropped through the foliage of the smaller trees and hit the forest floor within two feet of the spot where my dad stood, the same spot where he had picked up the first piece of fresh cutting. It was followed by another piece or two, and soon the pieces of husk seemed to rain down.

My dad motioned that he could see the squirrel but seemed to be telling me that he did not think he could kill it with the shotgun he carried. Later he said he figured he would get a better shot when the squirrel had finished the nut it was eating and went to the end of a limb to get another nut.

My dad did not get a shot when this happened, however, and the squirrel went back to the same place, on a limb that must have been four inches in diameter, to eat the nut. I saw the squirrel move, but with my little single-shot .22-caliber Springfield, I could not chance a moving shot. When it returned to the big limb I could not see it.

This happened again without either of us getting a shot, and my dad motioned me to come back to the spot where he stood.

When we were together again directly beneath the squirrel, my dad told me he could see the squirrel's chin protruding over the limb it sat on but didn't think the shotgun would do the job.

"Think you can hit something that small at this distance?"

he whispered. It was straight up, a terribly awkward position for shooting a rifle.

"I'll try," I said, dropping to one knee and cocking the little rifle.

Seconds later the rifle cracked and the squirrel dropped straight down. It nearly hit me.

Learning to interpret the stories nutshells tell about squirrels has served me well many times since.

Jack Cain, another of the old masters with whom I studied the fine art of squirrel hunting, once put on a clinic, which I took pretty much for granted at the time but which I now consider one of the finest demonstrations of squirrel-hunting savvy I have ever seen.

Jack and I entered the woods together just at daylight. It was the first woods we came to as we walked east from Crothersville through the fields toward the Muscatatuck River bottoms.

Ordinarily at daylight one can count on having almost no wind, but on this morning the wind was turning the leaves over a bit. That meant we would have to depend more on seeing the cuttings drop than hearing them if we expected to locate squirrels before we were nearly under them. The rustle of wind-blown leaves tends to render a squirrel hunter's sense of hearing almost useless.

Most good squirrel hunters will stop and stand motionless for several minutes—even sit down or lean against a tree—upon entering a woods at daylight. It more or less gives the hunter a chance to form a plan, not to mention the possibilities of seeing, hearing or otherwise locating a squirrel nearby.

We were within a few feet of each other when we stopped. I slid down to a sitting position with my back against a little white oak tree. Jack leaned against a small hickory. For some time we remained motionless. Finally

Jack motioned for me to come to the point where he stood.

"There's a squirrel in that little hickory by the beech den," he said, pointing to the east from the spot where we stood. "And there's another in that hickory to the left over by that pinoak. Which one do you want to get?"

I wasn't at all picayunish in those days—I never saw a squirrel I didn't want to hunt—so I said I would take the one on the hickory by the pinoak. I figured it would be less likely to get into a hole if it spooked.

We made our separate stalks and, though it was not planned, made our shots within a few seconds of each other. It didn't usually take more than one shot for either of us in those days.

I picked up my squirrel and sneaked to the point where Jack stood after picking up his.

"How'd you know those squirrels were there?" I asked. "I didn't see or hear either of them." I knew, of course, that he could not have heard the cuttings falling because of the wind.

"I didn't see or hear the squirrels either," Jack said, explaining that he could see the cuttings falling through openings in the trees where the rays of the sun were shining brightly.

It was a perfect demonstration of Jack's theory on hunting toward the sun when it is low, early in the morning and late in the afternoon. I have not forgotten that lesson either.

My dad taught me the same basic lesson in squirrel hunting and in almost the same manner, but on this occasion the sun was sinking in the afternoon and the squirrel he found was cutting poplar seed pods high in a huge yellow poplar (tulip) tree.

We had met in a big bottom woods and were quietly discussing the possibilities of heading for home—there wasn't much daylight left—when I realized that something other than our conversation had caught my dad's attention.

"I think we'd better go kill the squirrel on that big poplar before we go home," my dad said, pointing to the tree, which was a good sixty yards from the spot where we stood.

He pointed to a swath of sunlight streaming into the woods from the west and asked if I could see the individual poplar seeds whirligigging their way to the forest floor. On most of their way to the ground no human eye could have picked them up, but when they came through the swath of sunlight they seemed to be magnified.

My dad whispered that he did not know where the squirrel might be, but he suspected it was high in the tree. We approached from different directions and he was right. His shotgun boomed and down came the squirrel.

Over the years I have seen and heard of the importance of hickory nuts as a primary source of food for squirrels many times. If there is a tree in a woods that bears exceptionally good nuts, or if hickory trees are scarce—as they sometimes are—squirrels will come there to feed from all directions.

My dad used to tell the story about killing thirteen gray squirrels on one hickory at one time in the hill country east of Crothersville in Scott County, and this is a perfect example of the lure that a good hickory tree holds for squirrels.

This, of course, came in the days before wild game had much protection in Indiana.

My dad probably was on speaking terms with the hickory in question—a tall, thin tree that towered above all the other trees on the hillside. This hickory provided one limb which served as the sole escape route to a shorter but large beech tree. The beech in turn served as a squirrels' den. Thus, any squirrels that were congregated on the hickory to feed would have to travel along that lone limb to escape to the beech tree—either that or run down the trunk of the tree to the ground or simply bail out, which gray squirrels often do without hesitation.

To make conditions even more difficult—or easy, as it turned out—my dad knew there was only one place to stand where he could see much—about four feet—of the hickory limb. From anywhere else he would be shooting at gray blurs.

He was not surprised when he found the hickory literally crawling with gray squirrels soon after daylight and sneaked his way to the choice spot.

My dad said one gray was cutting a hickory nut on the bottom limb of the hickory—a true gray squirrel lookout characteristic. He shot it first. That touched off a wild scramble by the other squirrels, and my dad bagged twelve more as they crossed that four-foot span.

He said there were gray squirrels everywhere, but he concentrated on the limb that served as a bridge to the beech tree. When the shooting was over he could stand in one spot and pick up twelve of the squirrels. He had no idea how many times he shot the old Winchester Model 97, but he was good enough with it to connect on every shot—a welcome turn of events in those Depression days.

Killing thirteen squirrels on one day may sound a bit game-hoggish and irresponsible in these days of frozen dinners and microwaves, but when this incident occurred during the Depression no wild game taken was ever wasted. Not to mention the fact that there was far more game in those days and far fewer hunters.

One great feature of the hickory nut—in terms of providing both food for squirrels and hunting opportunities for outdoorsmen—is that it is a year-round thing.

Squirrel hunting is permitted in Indiana only between the middle of August and the end of December, but squirrels store mature hickory nuts for use in the winter and when they are doing this the hunter must alter his hunting techniques to meet the changing conditions.

Squirrels feed on hickory nuts throughout the year, but when the nuts start maturing in September or October—depending upon the tree involved—much of the day's activities involve the storing of nuts. By this time nights are cooler and squirrels—especially fox squirrels—do not rise with the crack of dawn. Instead they remain snug in their nests and dens, warding off the chill of night, until after the sun has risen. At this time of year they feed early in the morning and late in the afternoon; between times they bury nuts—one nut to each shallow hole in the forest floor.

My dad taught me all this—or rather interpreted what the nutshells told him—on a Sunday afternoon late in October back in the days when the squirrel season opened at mid-August and closed at mid-October. We were hickory nut hunting in the Muscatatuck River bottoms and there was one tree in particular that he wanted to go to.

Hickory nuts were not so plentiful that year as they often were, but he knew that this large sprangling hickory at the edge of a large woods offered a good crop because he had killed several squirrels there during the season.

When we arrived at the tree we found a lot of the green outer husks of hickory nuts on the ground but few of the hard inner shells.

My first thought was that someone else had picked up the nuts. My dad rejected that idea immediately, insisting that we had been beaten all right, but by squirrels, not by other hickory nut hunters.

To prove his point we backed off thirty or forty yards and sat with our backs to a big white oak tree. In the next twenty minutes three squirrels went to the tree on the ground to get nuts, which they carried off and buried.

When the third squirrel had left, my dad whispered that a hunter could sit right there and kill his limit.

Although we did not get any hickory nuts there, I may have learned more about squirrels in that twenty minutes than in any other short period of my life. I have seen the conditions we found under that hickory tree many times since then, and on many of those occasions I have backed off to find a comfortable place to sit—with gun in hand.

I don't think I have ever hunted squirrels in this manner without remembering the mini-lesson in squirrel behavior my dad taught me.

The Currect Way to Hunt

"HE'S HOT ON THIS ONE, BOYS," my dad said. "Let's get up there before the squirrel gets in a den."

"He" in this case was a cur dog named Ed, but we called him Ol' Ed in keeping with southern Indiana nomenclature tradition.

It is with more than a little reluctance that I leave the chase at this exciting point, but there is something that should be explained right here. You see, everything and everybody is Ol' this or Ol' that in many parts of southern Indiana, the "Ol'" being a sort of good ol' country prefix—an endearing term. It has nothing to do with one's age.

I was Ol' Bill Scifres when I was eight years old, and more than fifty years later I still answer to that name, whether I am in Crothersville, Hong Kong or someplace in between. I often identify myself in this manner out of force of habit.

Now, back to the chase.

We couldn't see it, but by the tempo of Ol' Ed's yowling it was obvious that he could smell the fat fox squirrel he was chasing so strongly that he could almost taste it. We were certain, though, that the squirrel was aware by now that there was trouble in the wind and would be heading for a den tree (one with a hollow limb or trunk) or at least a big tree with squirrel nests.

My dad was right, as he almost always was when he talked about hunting and fishing. In no more than a minute or two the frenzied barking smoothed out into long bawls, and that was what he had expected.

"He's treed," my dad said. "Let's get going."

With that my dad and my older brother, known (like my dad) as Jake through most of his life, broke into a gait that was right next to a run. In trying to keep pace, I was pelted in the face and body by limb after limb as they came flying back after being pulled forward and released.

That was part of the game, though, and in a few minutes my dad and brother stopped and started looking up into a large pinoak tree which stood near the edge of the thicket.

"No holes in that tree," my dad said. "No nests, either. We ought to be able to find this one."

Without further ado—we all knew what to do next—the three of us moved out from the trunk of the big pinoak in different directions and silently scanned the limbs of the tree while Ol' Ed continued to vent his ire at squirrels in general, with bawls that were shorter and shorter and came less and less frequently. But he knew that squirrel was there, and so did we.

Slowly the three of us rotated around the tree with necks craned backward and eyes searching the tree limb by limb and fork by fork from top to bottom.

"I think I see him," my dad said finally. "Come over here with that rifle, Bill."

I walked to my dad's side and he pointed out the squirrel with the business end of the Winchester Model 97 sixteen-gauge shotgun he carried.

"See him?" he asked. "All you can see is his ear and a little of the head. Think you can hit him?"

I said I would try and backed off to a small sapling I could use to steady the little rifle.

Try I did, but hit him I did not.

At the crack of the rifle, however, the squirrel ran up a large limb and prepared to jump into another tree. Just before the jump my dad's shotgun exploded and the squirrel fell dead.

Brother Jake got the squirrel away from Ol' Ed to keep him from chewing it up—we were not out there to feed the dog—and my dad slipped it into the back of his hunting coat.

With that bit of action over, Ol' Ed hied off through the brush. We just stood there for a while to see which direction we would go next. Ol' Ed would make that decision for us.

On that early October afternoon the three of us bagged only four squirrels. Ol' Ed "barked treed" fourteen times that afternoon, and I do not doubt that there was a squirrel up there someplace at every tree. Some were in inside dens, others in nests. It was a matter of squirrel hunting ethics, even in those days, that the real hunters did not bother squirrels when they were in a den or nest. Today it is law, at least in Indiana.

When fried up with hot biscuits and gravy, fried potatoes (with onion, of course), some boiled beans, fresh corn on the cob, sliced tomatoes and cucumbers from the garden, four squirrels made a fair "mess" for our family of seven (this included my grandmother, Missouri Dobbs). We had no complaints on Ol' Ed's performance.

I have since hunted squirrels over some dogs with which

one could expect a better percentage of shots per "tree," but four squirrels out of fourteen "trees" was not a bad average (roughly a 2.85 success ratio, if you are a stickler for statistics).

It might be of interest to the casual reader if I would digress from the original thesis of this story to point out another strange quirk in dog-naming procedures in small towns of southern Indiana.

You see, there was nothing whimsical about the naming of Ol' Ed. We obtained the dog—a duke's mixture with a lot of collie and black and tan hound in his veins—from a man named Ed Potts. I say "obtained" because I do not know whether we bought Ol' Ed or if he might have been a gift.

Another example of this practice of naming dogs for their former masters was a little wire-haired terrier (pretty close to straight stock, we thought) with the name of Debby. He was owned by a man named Deb (probably Delbert) Thomas, who lived on the west side of Crothersville.

My dad worked on the west side of town and struck up more than a nodding acquaintance with Debby. As a result, Debby often waited outside the factory where my dad worked and would come home with him.

Eventually Debby spent more time at our house than he did with his master. My dad finally bought him.

Debby, incidentally, was one of the best all-around hunting dogs we ever had.

"That dog would run anything that left a track," my dad used to say, long after Debby was no more. While I was not old enough to actually see Debby's deeds of derring-do in field and wood, I would listen as long as my dad would talk about their hunts. I would today if I could.

One of the best-remembered stories about Debby's hunting revolved around a Thanksgiving in the late 1920s—probably 1929.

My dad had gone hunting the day before Thanksgiving to get some rabbits—and perhaps some quail—for our holiday dinner.

My mother and my grandmother waited with much anticipation for his return because his success would more or less dictate the kind of Thanksgiving dinner we would have. There still would be time to run downtown the three or four blocks to the grocery store to get an old hen for baking, should my dad's hunt fail. But an old hen would be the best we could hope for—few people in Crothersville enjoyed the luxury of a Thanksgiving turkey in those days.

They couldn't believe their eyes when my dad came in late in the afternoon and started shucking game out of the back of his hunting coat. First there were rabbits and quail and finally five mallard ducks.

Debby was the star of the show, my dad said, because he not only found several of the quail after they dropped but also retrieved all of the ducks, even though the Muscatatuck River, into which they had fallen, was partially frozen and very hazardous.

Our Thanksgiving dinner was a raging success.

Debby died when I was five or six years old—the first real tragedy in my life. We could never substantiate the facts, but everything pointed to poison. How it was dispensed, and by whom, could not be determined, and that probably was best for all parties concerned.

A number of cur dogs came into my life before and after Jack Cain started making a bird hunter out of me, but they all were pretty much the same—a mixture of just about every breed one could imagine, with just enough hound blood in their veins to give them whatever it takes for a dog to smell a hot track. Some blood from the pointing breeds also helped some of them.

That, of course, is the strong suit of curs. They do not

have the nose to run a cold track, and as a result any time they start barking on track the game is only minutes ahead.

I have heard coon and fox hounds mince around over cold tracks for more than an hour, only to lose the track eventually and have to start all over again. I do not fault these dogs for what they do—a pack of potlickers can make beautiful music when they straighten out a track.

As a matter of fact, Jim Ramsey, photo editor of the *Indianapolis Star* until his retirement a few years back, his son, Brent, and I used to join John Olson (deer biologist), Jerry Wise (grouse and wild turkey biologist), and Larry Lehman (fur-bearer biologist) every year for a long weekend of hunting on the opening weekend of the upland game seasons.

We would set up a camp in the large wilderness area east of Monroe Reservoir where we could hunt just about everything in season. We always fared pretty well on these trips in terms of hunting success, but one of the highlights of the weekend for me would be going to sleep at night.

I always took my little trail tent and a large Coleman sleeping bag that just about filled the floor of the tent.

Clover, an English setter of which you will hear more later in this book, would come in to sleep at my feet, and our lullaby would be the concert provided by a pack of coon hounds sending Mr. Ringtail over the wooded hills.

Still, for hunting squirrels and some of the fur-bearing animals at night, a hot-nosed cur is hard to beat.

Another of our curs that turned out very well was Ol' Ring (he was named before we got him).

Ol' Ring would tree squirrels by day just as well as Ol' Ed, but he also doubled as the resident possum dog. He would run a raccoon if he chanced across a hot track.

Raccoons were not real plentiful in those days. Hunters with good hounds would catch eight or ten coon a year.

Today a year's take for the same hunters and dogs could be unlimited. Eight or ten raccoons might be a one-night bag.

We didn't catch many raccoons with our cur dogs, but one of my favorite outdoor experiences usually started at the kitchen table when we had finished supper and my dad and I would be talking as he finished his last cup of coffee.

"This would be a good night to get some possums to eat," he would say, blowing the coffee in his saucer to cool it.

He would wash and polish the globe of the lantern and we would pull on our boots and head out the west side of town with the dog—Ol' Ed or Ol' Ring—tugging at the chain until we were across U.S. 31 and the Pennsylvania Railroad tracks. Released on the far side of the tracks, the dog would head for the fields and thickets, and we would hear no more until his barking told us there was action in the offing.

When the dog would bark treed we knew where he almost always would be—at one of several persimmon trees that dotted the fields. The possum likes persimmons just as much as the jokes and old sayings indicate.

When the dog would tree, we would go to him. If the possum was healthy looking—at least, as healthy as a possum can appear—I would hold the dog and my dad would hold his big five-cell flashlight along the barrel of my little rifle and fetch him down with a shot in the head. But in addition to being presentable, the possum had to be about half to two-thirds grown and nice and fat.

When we had two or three good eating possums, the hunt would end.

Back home, I would hold the possums while my dad skinned them. He would give the pelts to me to sell to the fur buyer, but he took extra precautions with the carcasses because we used them for food.

The thought of eating a possum may be anything but pleasant to most folks for a variety of reasons. The most distasteful reason probably revolves around the fact that the possum—true to his reputation—will eat just about anything. Still, I don't look down my nose at fried chicken, and the chicken will eat just about anything, too. Anyhow, even though the possum tends to fulfill his role of scavenger, he also eats a great variety of other foods, including corn, persimmons and other fruits.

My dad always said there are two important things to remember in preparing a possum for the table. The first was the removal of as much of the body fat as possible; the second was to use a lot of pepper when frying or baking the meat.

When rolled in flour and fried with onions, possums were as good as any meat we had—wild or domestic.

The meat of the possum is not dark like raccoon or muskrat but more like the thighs of chicken. I have heard many of the old-timers at Crothersville say it was "as close to turtle as you can get without having turtle."

The Making of a Bird Dog

AT FIRST I COULDN'T believe it, but there stood Pokey—on as staunch a point as a self-styled bird dog trainer could ask. I did not doubt there were quail there.

Pokey, the English setter whose real name was Skyrocket's Polka Dot, was not yet two years old, but there she was on point just after daylight on a November morning in 1956.

My wife, Nancy, and I had driven down to Austin on Sunday afternoon, the preceding day, and had spent the night with my sister and her husband, Mr. and Mrs. Freeman Chandler. Freeman and Mick lived east of Austin on his old home place. It was smack in the middle of bird country and only a mile or so from the old Muscatatuck River bottoms, where I had grown up hunting birds with William Branard (Jack) Cain and Duke, the dropper (half setter, half pointer), which probably was the best bird dog I have ever hunted over.

I had hoped Freeman would be able to hunt with me on this, my first serious day of hunting with Pokey, but it was not to be. He was working days and with a family growing up could not afford to take the time off.

"You take old Gypsy and you'll find plenty of birds for that pup to work," he said. Although I was grateful for the offer to loan me his English setter, I could not accept.

To my way of thinking, taking another man's dog hunting would be as bad as using his toothbrush. I would not allow anyone else to take my dog hunting if I could not go, and I would not expect anyone else to feel differently about the matter.

I don't even like to intervene in the rapport another hunter has with his dog when I am hunting with them, except for a "steady" or "fetch" command, something very simple that I have heard the dog's owner use.

At any rate, there we were—a green pup and a hunter full of expectations. The sun was setting the horizon ablaze across the corn stubble fields to the east, and the little twenty-gauge Winchester Model 50 was stuffed with light loads of No. 8s.

Pokey was on point in a little patch of ragweed and what I call "tickle grass" because it is low and thick and often works its way up my trouser legs. It was a perfect place for a covey of quail to roost, and with the frost still on I knew this covey had not yet moved.

"Steady, girl," I told her as I moved in to flush the birds. At the same time I was telling myself that it was not important that I kill a lot of birds on the rise, but that it was important that I bring down one and make sure it was dead. I didn't want Pokey to be confronted with the task of trying to find a wing-tipped cripple that was running all over the place.

So when the covey exploded and headed for the big thicket some forty yards to the north, I took my time, picked out a rooster bird and fired a single shot. The bird crumpled, and I watched it down in the weeds a good ten yards from the edge of the thicket.

"Hunt dead!" I commanded, but I didn't really need to say that. Pokey had watched the bird fall and was headed for the spot.

She didn't find the bird immediately, and I wanted to get in there and help her several times. I managed to restrain myself, though, and when she finally found the bird I ordered her to "fetch." She would have no part of that.

She did pick up the bird, turn to show me that she had it, drop it again and stand at the spot until I got there to pick it up. I was not unhappy at that performance.

"What the hell," I thought, "I can force-break her to retrieve later."

With that bird in my hunting coat and twenty to twenty-five others scattered down the east side of the thicket, I stopped to think it over.

I called Pokey in, put the leash on her and sat down beside a big white oak tree at the edge of the thicket. Then I fired up my pipe and took a rest I didn't need.

Fifteen minutes later, when I figured the birds had settled down in the thicket, I put away my pipe and turned Pokey loose to hunt again. By talking to her and giving her hand signals I managed to keep her along the east side of the thicket, where I was almost sure we would find the singles. We were at the north end of the thicket—about a quarter of a mile from the spot where we had found the covey—before Pokey showed any signs of being "birdy" again.

"She's found a single," I told myself a few minutes later as I waded through the briers and brush where she was on point. But when the action came it was not a single bird—it was another covey, and Pokey flushed them wild (probably because they were running). There were at least as many birds—perhaps even more—than there were in the first bunch.

"BLAM! BLAM!" the little shotgun spoke, and another bird dropped. Poked found this one, too, but she would not retrieve.

At that point I made a decision which probably was the making of Pokey.

"I will not shoot another bird unless she points and holds it!" I told myself emphatically. I kept my word. I didn't want her to develop the bad habit of moving in on birds even if I was close enough to shoot. I figured I could, and should, flush the birds.

On a number of occasions that day singles and doubles would flush from the deep cover of dry leaves in the thicket before Pokey could get close enough (or get enough scent) to go on point. In other encounters she would be on point, but the birds would flush before I was in close behind her.

I could have dropped a lot of those birds, but I didn't fire, even though I had to almost fight myself at times to avoid it. I wanted a limit of birds that day as badly as I have ever wanted anything.

When Pokey pointed birds I tried to kill them, but even with No. 10 shot I was shooting at a disadvantage in the dense thicket. There were a lot of misses.

We rested several times during the long day—including our lunch break when we shared my sandwiches.

When we left the thicket just before dark I had a limit of ten quail in the back of my hunting coat and a very tired bird dog.

Freeman and I wheeled into his driveway at about the same time, and he couldn't believe I had killed a limit of birds with a pup that was hunting for what really was her first time out. But the proof was there.

It was a day to remember, all the more so now because

both Pokey and that big thicket have been gone for many years.

Two of the hunting incidents involving Pokey that I remember best occurred on the Muscatatuck River and either could have spelled disaster—or worse—for both of us.

We hunted the bottomlands—even the banks—of the old Muscatatuck, because that is where I grew up. I was almost on speaking terms with many of the coveys of quail that lived there because I had been hunting most of them since I had started hunting quail with Jack Cain at about the age of eleven. Outlaws tend to return to the scene of the crime, they say, and bird hunters are no different. Success takes the bird hunter back to those favored spots time after time.

Pokey's "coming out," of course, was many years after I had moved away from Crothersville, but it was well before the completion of I-65, the superhighway south from Indianapolis, so we almost always would leave home at 2:30 or 3:00 A.M. to make the three-hour drive to Jackson County and have some time for breakfast before starting the hunt soon after sunup. Because my days off in those days were Sunday and Monday and hunting was taboo on the former, Pokey and I often had to go it alone. Jack Cain's eyes were not what they once had been and he no longer could stand the gaff of an all-day hunt. Now and then he would join me for a few hours—he loved to watch Pokey hunt—but many of the best hunts we had involved only the two of us, one man and one dog who understood and respected each other.

One day when we were soloing the big bottomland thickets of the Tobias Bridge area (the old rickety bridge, as my kids called it because the floor planks played a tune when we crossed), we scattered a large covey of birds along the brush-infested banks of the river. The river, which was five or six feet above normal and very muddy and swift, was bordered by a maple-ash-pinoak thicket that probably was two hundred yards long and fifty yards wide, and the birds had scattered there. We later would find that many of the birds were sitting within ten or twelve yards of the water, and that caused a problem.

Unless we wanted to walk all the way to Tobias Bridge, then back to this spot, we could shoot no birds that were not clearly over the bank we were hunting. Dropping a bird in the water would have been real trouble.

All went well for a time. Pokey was finding the singles like clockwork and I was shooting just about as well. Occasionally a bird would flit out over the water or go to the far bank, but when this occurred I would assure Pokey things would get better and the hunt would go on.

Then it happened, just as I feared it might. Pokey pointed a single, and it presented a perfect straightaway shot parallel to the river. Easy game, Coach. But when I fired, the bird veered sharply to the left and dropped in the middle of the river.

I didn't expect Pokey to go into the swift water, but she saw the bird splash and was after it before I could stop her.

I was concerned—justifiably so—but Pokey made it look easy. Never before had she retrieved a bird, but she fought the swift water to get to this one and headed back toward the high, steep bank where I stood yelling encouragement.

All went well until she got within about three feet of the bank. There the current had pushed a small willow down into the water parallel to the shore, and she had to cross it.

With the bird in her mouth she would get her front feet up on the flimsy willow trying to cross it, but the current would catch her hips and back legs and start to sweep her under.

After she had made two or three attempts I tried to call her to other spots, but she was confused by my frantic instructions. Worse yet, the current was making her tired.

Finally, in desperation I placed my gun beside a tree and slid down the steep bank on heels and posterior. I drove my right heel into the bank at the edge of the water, planted the left foot solidly as I grasped a one-inch elm sapling with my right hand and leaned far out over the swift water to grab Pokey's collar with my left hand.

I pulled Pokey over the willow and pushed her up the bank while going in over both knee boots. Then, planting one heel after the other deep in the mud, I backtracked up the bank to safety.

The dead bird—which had not entered my mind for several minutes—awaited me at the top of the bank.

On another occasion, a six-inch snow and zero temperatures hit southern Indiana the weekend before the last day of the bird season on Monday, but Pokey and I were trying a final hunt even though conditions were anything but ideal.

Again we were hunting those bottomland thickets in the Tobias Bridge area, but this time without much luck. Birds hadn't moved in the near-zero temperatures.

After crossing the river several times on ice and following the banks closely to get to another thicket, I missed Pokey.

The hope that springs eternal within bird hunters told me at first that she probably was on point nearby and that I soon would find her. But when a quick search revealed nothing, I remembered that two or three hundred yards upstream we had passed a spot in the river where the current had maintained a stretch of open water in the middle of the river. It was not wide—no more than ten feet—but it had ice all around it, and if Pokey had gotten in there we were in one big jam.

I ran back to the spot and sure enough, Pokey was

trapped. When I would call her she would get one or both front feet on the ice, but I knew this was hopeless. She could not get out by herself.

To make matters worse, the ice obviously was too thick for Pokey to break, but I doubted that it would support my weight.

Still, Pokey's life was in my hands and I could see that she was getting tired.

Again I stashed my shotgun against a tree and again I slid down the bank to the ice, which had frozen since the snow had hit. The ice supported my weight at the edge of the banks, but I could feel it giving a step or two out and dropped first to my hands and knees, then to my belly as water oozed through.

The ice didn't break, though, and with a swimming, scooting motion I eased out toward open water until I could reach Pokey's collar. Then with one strong effort I pulled her onto the ice.

I was turning around and scooting for the shore again when Pokey celebrated her return to safety by shaking vigorously, showering me with ice water.

Back on the high bank I pulled a leash from the back of my hunting coat and, with clothes freezing, led Pokey back to the car.

It was—in at least one important way—one of the best ends I had ever seen for a bird season.

Skyrocket's Polka Dot (Kanzequity Boy-Jessie's Judy), always Pokey to us, was bred by the late George B. Allen. She was whelped on March 23, 1955, but was almost four months old before she came to our house, soon after we moved to Trail's End on the banks of White River.

How she got there is yet another story.

In trying to produce a well-rounded outdoor column, I started writing about bird dogs and field trial results soon after "Lines and Shots" started appearing on the sports page of the *Indianapolis Star*. But I did not have a dog at the time.

On a late winter day in 1955, while I was talking with several members of the Indiana Field Trial Association, one of the dog men asked if I would like to have a dog.

My answer was in the affirmative, of course, and the next question I faced was "What kind of dog would you like?"

"Well," I said, "I would want a female English setter with a lot of black spots and/or ticking and I would prefer the runt of a litter."

For several seconds the dog men, all good field trialers and bird hunters, looked at each other with puzzled expressions, not saying anything. Then someone in the group said, "Hell, we give away dogs like that."

"Why do you want a dog like that?" somebody said.

"I want the female runt," I said, "because it usually is the smartest of the litter. The runt has to be smart to survive. I like the ticking or black spots because I like to see a dog well marked."

"We're not kiddin'," somebody said. "We give away dogs like that."

By then I was beginning to suspect that I would be back in the bird dog business sooner than I expected. Furthermore, I figured my pup would be gratis, and I didn't want that. I did want another bird dog. I hadn't owned a dog since I hied off to Hanover College in the fall of 1948, and I missed it something miserable.

In conversations with field trialers and bird hunters in the next few weeks I learned that Allen, who lived at Bandana, Kentucky, a stone's throw from Monkey's Eyebrow, had English setter stock that was hard to beat.

I wrote to George, telling him my preferences, and we had a telephone call soon thereafter. The gist of the conversation was that his Jessie's Judy would be whelping any day and that he would keep an eye peeled for a pup that he thought would meet my needs, mainly bird hunting. I was not remotely interested in field trialing, even though I found it interesting.

Two or three weeks later I had a letter from George. He was sure he had a pup out of Jessie's Judy that I would like. But he didn't want to sell it to me until it was about four months old.

The deal was sealed. I could have this pup for seventy-five dollars, and he would send her Railway Express to Indianapolis when he thought the time was right. He emphasized that I should not pay him unless I was satisfied with the pup.

George called toward the middle of July, soon after we moved into the house on the river, to tell me he had shipped the pup and that I should check daily with the Railway Express office to see if she had arrived. He didn't want her confined to her small shipping cage any longer than necessary.

Four or five days later the new puppy arrived, skinny, awkward and scared to death. I picked her up at the freight yard. It was my day off, and I fancied that we would have some fun getting to know each other when we got home.

That was not to be. When I pried the top of the wire cage off and lifted the trembling puppy out onto the floor of the utility area in the garage, she ran behind the washer. No amount of sweet talking or hamburger would lure her out. Several times I pulled her gently from her hiding place and put her down, but she always went back to her sanctuary. There wasn't even enough space behind the washer for her to lie down and certainly nothing more comfortable than concrete and a maze of pipes and rubber hoses.

Finally I gave up and left her there with the garage doors closed. I certainly didn't want her to get away.

After a day or so she started coming out from behind the washer to eat, but she was still terribly frightened. I blamed the train ride of four or five days. I didn't see how it could have been anything else.

I vowed I would never have another animal sent anyplace by common carrier, and I have lived up to that vow. I hope I can always stick to it.

As Pokey got more familiar with her new surroundings—the garage, the fenced-in back yard and yes, the house—she became more and more friendly and soon was housebroken. That meant she could come in the house and stay as long as she liked.

Since Nancy and I had no children during the first five years, Pokey became almost an only child. I would be home in the daytime—even on workdays—and Nancy would be home from late afternoon on through the evening.

Pokey became the happiest, most loving and most loved dog I have ever owned. She loved the runs we took in the field by day, and she was not averse to the life she lived at night.

About the time Pokey became one year old I started running her with an old English setter named Tony, which was owned by the late Clarence Lowe, for many years manager of the County Line Dock at Geist Reservoir.

Clarence would call when he had an hour or two of free time and would swing past the house. We would walk out into the fields with the dogs from the house on Trail's End. No need to go anyplace else in those days to find birds—I could sit on my front porch and hear the "bobwhite" song, even see quail. It was a symphony like no other.

When Donna, our first daughter, arrived in the spring of 1960 Pokey was well established at our house, both as a bird dog and as the family pet.

Pokey had the run of the house and a fenced-in back yard when she cared to be there.

She spent most of the' day in the house with me and most of the evenings with Nancy. When bedtime came, she slept on a throw rug on the floor at my side of the bed. After Nancy left for work, she slept on the bed, at times with her head on Nancy's pillow, just as a person would sleep.

We also had a number of cats and kittens—thanks to the old calico cat named Puss, who came to our house via the home of Kay and George B. Steel Jr. Although Pokey would allow the cats to be on the bed when I was sleeping in the mornings—it usually was about 3 A.M. when I got home from work—they could not be above my waist. For a cat to venture too close to my chest and head was sure trouble.

Nancy could tell when it was time for me to be getting home. As if stirred by some built-in alarm, Pokey would awaken from her spot beside the bed and go sit backward in a large chair that overlooked the open fields through the living room picture window.

Ellers Road ran a north-south course to 116th Street far across the fields—well over a quarter of a mile—and Pokey would watch the headlights of the cars on that road. She showed nothing—just looked intently—as the occasional car moved up the road. But when my car passed, Pokey's tail would wag and Nancy knew I would be home in a matter of minutes.

Pokey didn't just hunt and while away the home hours with me. She did many of the things I did outdoors. Once while fishing from a boat at Geist Reservoir I hauled in a nice bass and the lure flipped out as I lifted the fish into the boat. While I was trying to keep the bass from flopping out of the boat Pokey grabbed the lure. Fortunately I got the lure away from her before she was hooked.

Thus, one of the first things we talked about the day I brought Nancy and Donna home from the hospital was what Pokey might think about the arrival of a child. The answer was not long in coming.

Pokey had given the baby a wide berth throughout the afternoon that day, so after dinner we decided the time was ripe to get the two acquainted.

With Donna in her new bassinet (it stood waist high) in the middle of the living room, I carried in a kitchen chair and motioned Pokey to jump up where she could see the baby.

Dutifully, Pokey did my bidding. But she would not look at Donna. Her glum look left no doubt that she was bored with the entire proceedings and probably more than a little jealous.

That brought much concern to both Nancy and me. We could not have a child and a dog competing for our affections.

"Well," one of us said, "we'll just have to shower Pokey with affection . . . let her know that she still is important to all of us."

That we did. As a result, before our problem had a chance to develop it had disappeared. Pokey still slept on the rug at my side of the bed, but the bassinet was there, too.

When Donna was old enough to sleep in her own baby bed in her own room, an interesting bond seemed to develop. When we would put Donna to bed at night, Pokey would follow and lie down by the side of the bed. She would stay there until Donna was asleep, then walk to the open door and emit a quiet little "woof, woof" sound, which we interpreted as her way of telling us Donna was asleep and asking permission to come back to the living room. Permission was always granted.

If Donna awakened, Pokey went back to resume her bed-side vigil. Likewise, she would quit her slumbers at my bed-side to go to Donna's room if she should awaken in the night.

When Donna was old enough to toddle around outside, our front yard was not yet fenced. But it didn't matter. If another dog or any other animal or person should be in the yard with Donna, Pokey was always between them.

Pokey would spend evenings in the living room with us, usually snoozing under a coffee table at the end of the couch and adjacent to a large, comfortable chair, which more or less was my throne. Occasionally Pokey would jump up in the chair with me (with or without an invitation) and turn around with her back to the back of the chair, just as I sat.

Pokey and I played one game a lot. With Pokey snoozing under the end table, or whatever else she might be doing, I would say, "Pokey, I think you'd better go to the kitchen."

When she was there I would tell her, "Now lie down." The next sound would be Pokey plopping down on the kitchen floor.

I could send her to almost any room of the house and call her back when the notion suited me. She would stay where I sent her until I told her she could return.

Pokey did not always eat all of her food when she was fed, and as a result the cats sometimes helped polish it off. That led to one of the most remarkable examples of communication between dog and man I have ever seen.

Once, after we had eaten, Nancy fed Pokey and she scarcely touched her food. But an hour or so later I noticed Pokey asleep under the end table in the living room and her food dish—with almost all of the food in it—on the floor very close to her head.

Neither of us had seen Pokey carry the dish from the kitchen to the living room, but neither of us had placed it there—and that left Pokey. She had brought her food to the living room to keep the cats from getting it.

"Pokey," I said sternly, upon seeing the dish in the living room, "take that food back to the kitchen."

With no hesitation, Pokey got up, picked up the pan by its edge—apparently the same way she had carried it to the living room—and carried it back to the kitchen, where she ate the food. Then she came back to the living room and continued her respite.

Pokey always received a present—maybe several—at Christmas. One of the pictures we still view with fond memories has Nancy giving Pokey her present (a yellow box of Kennel Ration Treats) in the middle of the living room floor. In the picture Pokey is licking her chops as though she can hardly wait to open the box.

If Pokey's career produced an all-time low point, it probably came on her second Christmas Day.

We went to the home of Nancy's parents in Broad Ripple for Christmas dinner and Pokey was invited. After our late afternoon dinner, Nancy's dad separated the remaining meat from the bones of the turkey and had two big platters—one white meat and one dark meat—in the kitchen.

Somehow somebody left the kitchen door open while we all were resting in the living room, and Pokey slipped into the kitchen and helped herself to a goodly portion from that white meat platter.

I scolded her good, but if the truth were known I may have been smiling a little on the inside. I never was wild about white meat.

In short, Pokey was a part of almost everything we did at home.

To other hunters it probably wasn't noticeable, but Pokey started slowing up in the field and I started thinking in terms of another puppy. I knew it would have to come from George Allen. I had been so pleased with Pokey that another breeder would not even have been considered. Anyhow I liked the Skyrocket and Beau Essig's Don blood.

Pokey was in what I considered her fifth season—she was seven years old—at the time.

Being the procrastinator I have always been (my philosophy has always been that a body should not get too excited about anything today if he can get just as excited about it tomorrow), I let that season slide by without ordering a pup.

In the following year George didn't come up with anything he thought I would like but said he could refer me to several other breeders or make a special effort to get me a pup in the following year, if I would want to wait.

George called toward the end of January 1966 to say his bitch, Allen's Lady Equity, had been bred to Allen's Skyrocket Boy and that she had produced a litter of nine pups on the previous December 29.

"You can come down and pick your own, or I'll pick one for you," he told me on the telephone. He added that he figured they all would be there at least until early spring.

We drove down for two reasons. First, we did not want the pup to have to endure a train ride of several days. Secondly, I wanted to meet George and see his operation.

It was a seven-hour drive from our house to Bandana, but Nancy and I were there a little after noon. We talked with George and his family for a while as we got unkinked from the ride, then went out to look at the pups.

It was a beautiful April afternoon, and I relaxed in the lush grass while George pointed out several of his older dogs. He let his Lady dog out of the pen without a leash and kept her under perfect control, even though she had not been out of the pen since before she had her pups.

"I've been saving that little bitch for you," he said, pointing to a gangly, skinny pup. "I'll get her out and see what you think."

The pup came bursting out of the pen like a herd of wild mustangs. After a quick lap or two around the pen, she headed straight for the spot where I knelt on one knee in a large patch of Dutch clover.

She never put on the brakes but hit me full tilt in the chest and nearly bowled me over backwards. I wrapped my arms around her to try to calm her down, but this was the first real attention she had ever had from a human and she was enjoying it to the fullest.

Every fiber in her body was going double time—holding her was just about all I could do. There was no way I could defend myself against the barrage of sloppy kisses she was planting all over my face.

George got a leash on her and held her at bay while I regained my composure. Then we sat in that patch of clover and got to know each other even better while Nancy recorded the goings-on with a camera.

"Her name will be Skyrocket's Clover Girl," I told George.

Pokey's training as a puppy had been slow—mostly just runs in the fields with older dogs—but it was not that way with Clover. In the years since Pokey had been a pup I had read and talked with several dog trainers about sight-pointing techniques for puppies, so Clover and I were out in the front yard hard at work the next morning.

I tied one end of a piece of monofilament fishing line onto a seven-foot spinning rod and attached an old brown work glove to the other end. We went to work in the front yard, which by then had been fenced.

Things went just about the way I had been told they would. When I flipped the old glove out on the grass, Clover would charge, trying to get it. Now and then she did. But we played with that glove, and played some more, until finally she realized she could not get the glove with any regularity by chasing it. Then she went on point.

She would, of course, try to sneak in on the glove—one step at a time—until she could stand it no longer. Then she would make her lunge. But I always lifted it away just in time and we would start all over again.

That's the way it went for several days. But finally the words "whoa" and "steady" came to mean something. When that happened I could get Clover on point, place the fishing rod on the ground and walk over to sit in the shade after forming her up and lifting her tail skyward.

Still, when the cool days of fall came and I could start running Pokey and Clover together in the fields downstream from the house, the latter did not resemble a working gun dog in any way. There can be no doubt that Clover profited from her sessions with Pokey. The two got along fabulously, except when the pup was about to bust the old dog's birds. However, I had not been successful in teaching Clover to back another dog—she simply hadn't been into enough birds. As a result Pokey did the teaching.

When Pokey would be on point and Clover would insist on moving in until she could get her own whiff, Pokey would emit a low, throaty growl. That would stop Clover, but then she would be reluctant to join in the hunt for a few minutes. Only once, to my knowledge, did Pokey ever attack the pup physically, and that was over a dead bird. Later, I would see Clover do basically the same thing to another pup.

Clover did make a few points that first year, but generally she followed the path most English setters take. She didn't look much like a bird dog until her second season. Only a handful of bird dog men used live pen-raised birds in those days, and they, for the most part, were field trialers.

Clover came on strong toward the middle of her second season. With Pokey obviously slowing and able to hunt only half days, Clover was finding most of our birds. Pokey, of course, was nearing twelve years old.

Pokey still wanted to hunt, though, so I would hunt her at prime times of the day and at special places where I knew we would be into birds in a short time after we left the car. At other times, if the weather was suitable for leaving a dog in the car, I would leave Pokey there and hunt Clover alone.

I didn't bag nearly as many birds with that arrangement. But I was certain that Pokey would be unable to hunt the following year, and Clover needed all the exposure to birds I could give her if she were to become a bird dog.

She had a good nose—there could be no doubt about that—but she was the hardest-headed dog I had ever tried to train. Even as a two-year-old she had a knack for doing whatever she pleased, regardless of my commands. This habit seemed to worsen in the next two years.

Pokey remained the dominant dog in the house. But Clover came in the house when she wanted to and was part of the family. Except on nights that were very cold she slept in the garage until after Pokey was gone.

Going bird hunting and returning, Pokey would sit in the front seat of the old Jeep Wagoneer or snooze on my hunting coat while I picked burs from places she could not reach. Clover would ride in the back seat. But neither of my dogs ever rode in a cage or the back of a pickup truck unless I was there with them.

There were, of course, many memorable hunts in the two seasons I was able to hunt Pokey and Clover together. But the best hunt of all—at least the one I remember best— came on the last day of the bird season in 1967 when Pokey was running out the string.

We had gone to Crothersville early that morning with the hope that my brother-in-law could go with us. He couldn't go, so I hunted both Pokey and Clover in the hills around his house until 10:30 or 11:00 A.M. By that time it was getting a little warm, so I put Pokey on the closed-in back porch where my sister, Maxine, could keep an eye on her and headed out again with Clover after lunch.

I still wanted to hunt the big Muscatatuck River bottoms at least part of the day, though, so about 3:00 P.M. we went back, picked up Pokey and stopped in the bottoms for the last two hours of the day and the season.

We headed around the thicket where Pokey and I had enjoyed her first great day as a bird dog. The wind picked up, the air temperature started falling and massive banks of dark clouds became visible in the west.

We skirted the west side of that thicket and went on to the high mound of earth where we always found birds. Still no success.

When it became obvious that we soon would be running out of daylight, we headed for the banks of little White Oak Creek to follow it the half-mile back to the car.

It was getting late when we neared the car. Ordinarily, under those circumstances, I would have called it a day. There was, after all, a storm coming in and I have never liked to scatter birds late in the afternoon when there is bad weather in the offing.

We would have quit on this day, too. But 150 yards before we reached the road both dogs got birdy along the brush-infested creek bank and I let them do their thing.

The dogs went up and down both banks, their tails fanning the brush and briers as they do only when they are hot on birds, but they couldn't find them. Soon they were off up the hillside, through an unpicked soybean patch and into a big ragweed patch on top of the hill.

I followed, thinking all the time that the birds would be on the roost in the ragweeds.

Both dogs went on point several times, but neither held long enough for me to get there. It was getting darker by the minute.

Finally, when it was almost too dark to shoot and I had not seen nor heard either dog for two or three minutes, I looked down a bushy draw toward the creek to see two whitish blurs standing very still.

There was no time to waste. I almost ran to the dogs— Pokey on a beautiful, solid point and Clover, five or six feet behind, on one of her forced backs. Pokey obviously had found the birds and had halted Clover in her tracks with a growl when she had tried to get too close.

I dropped two birds when they got up, both falling in the unpicked soybeans. Pokey found one and waited for me to come and get it. Clover brought in the other bird.

As I pocketed the birds Pokey was bouncing around like a pup—the adrenalin flows at exciting times in old dogs, it seems, just as it does in old men.

It was dark by the time I had the dogs settled in the car and traded knee boots for work shoes.

Standing beside the car and looking out across the river bottoms I could see the edge of the thicket where Pokey had pointed that first covey of birds on a frosty morning more than ten years before. We had parked no more than two hundred yards from the spot. In the other direction— about the same distance—I could see the spot where Pokey had found the birds half an hour or so earlier. It was not until then that I realized that Pokey's bird-hunting life had come in and gone out in a blaze of glory with the same covey of birds.

Just as Pokey was very much a part of Clover's training to hunt and her life through the first two years, she was just as absent from that time on. Pokey's death at age twelve made Clover the top dog—the only dog—both for hunting and as a family pet.

It was easy for Clover to move into the void Pokey's death left as the family pet, but it would take three more seasons for the pup to become even a semblance of Pokey the bird dog. And there were doubts that this would ever happen.

Clover had a great nose, but she could not be handled in the manner in which I work with dogs. It is very difficult for me to get really nasty to an animal that eats out of my hand under the table. Clover earned the title I gave her— the hardest-headed dog I ever saw.

This dog would botch up the handling of a covey of birds, and I would get right down in the field on top of her trying to make her do things my way. I would rant and rave, and call her everything in the book, even try to make her think I was beating her.

Clover would respond by getting up and doing the same thing again.

However, "Success breeds contentment," according to the old saw, and Clover's hunting star would shine just often enough for me to see her potential.

Much to my consternation, a cur Lothario, which ran the neighborhood on 111th Street where we had moved when Clover was four years old, would father a litter of six pups (two long-haired females and four short-haired males), named Dandy, Goldie, Patrick, Casey, Shawn, and Kelly before their eyes were opened. You see, they were born on St. Patrick's Day, 1971.

Pups were free at our house, but the qualifications for getting one were almost as stringent as those of a county adoption agency in the 1940s. To make matters worse, Dandy, the black and white long-haired female, sat up soon after she was born and put her front paw on Nancy's hand, and I found Goldie, the liver and white long-hair, the most cuddly thing I had ever seen.

We placed the four short-haired males and Goldie, but with the option of taking them back if our visitations indicated the dogs were not being treated properly. Eventually, we would exercise that option with Goldie and she would be our dog again (I was so happy) until she went to spend the rest of a long life with my brother, Jack, and his wife, Janet, who is Nancy's sister.

Dandy, incidentally, was well past her eighteenth birthday when we had to have her put to sleep only a few days before this was written in the summer of 1989. It was one very sad day.

I tell the story of Clover's lone litter of pups only because it had such profound effects on Clover. It was bad enough that the scroungy cur had availed himself of Clover while she was in my fenced-in back yard, but even worse when he returned the following winter.

This time I noticed the symptoms of Clover's impending blessed event and took her to Dr. Fleming and Dr. Ward, who explained that they could abort the litter of pups but that in so doing they would render Clover incapable of having puppies ever again.

"Thank God," I said, bidding them to get on with their work. I did not want another dog like Clover, I told myself— and that thought would come back to haunt me.

They cautioned me against over-feeding Clover after the operation because that could make her too fat to hunt. But everything went well, and when the next bird season rolled around I went to the field with a new dog. No longer did I need to scream my head off to get her to go where I wanted her to go or do what I wanted her to do—just point with my hand and arm and sweet talk her a little, like: "Find ol' birds, Dinky (one of several names I gave her)." And she would go do it. Moreover, she would hold them, she would retrieve, she would do just about anything I asked her to do except break a point and come to me when I called.

The transition seemed to come magically, almost as if I had flipped a switch to bring it all about.

I don't think Clover ever attained Pokey's covey-finding ability. But she got so laid back and cool when birds were scattered that I had to call her off the covey downstream from our old house in the river bottoms almost every year to keep from shooting them down too low in numbers. I did that with a lot of coveys. Clover was like an alarm clock on singles; she just perked around the cover until she got a whiff and went on point. She often would be locked up fifteen or twenty feet from a single bird but would move slowly toward the bird when I got behind her or at her side.

Obviously the surgery had changed Clover's personality completely, and the ratty mongrel that slipped over the fence and into the back yard with her was at least partially responsible. Still, had it not been for the fact that he looked the part of a very good squirrel dog, I could have hated him with a passion.

Clover's hunting stock soared even more a year or two later when Dan Gapen, the Minneapolis fishing tackle manufacturer, came down to hunt birds with me.

It was late in December and we had gone to the large area east of Monroe Reservoir. Toward the middle of the afternoon, when we both were worn down from fighting the brush and hills, I started Clover around the edge of a picked soybean patch in a long hollow completely bordered by brush and woods.

When we got about halfway down one side of the broad hollow Dan appeared to be pretty well bushed, so I suggested that he sit for a spell while I ran Clover to the end of the hollow and came back on the other side of the soybean field. I told Dan he could cut across the field to rejoin us on the way back.

Clover did not find any quail, but soon after Dan had joined us on the far side of the soybean patch, she went into a brush-filled draw and locked up.

"Let's be careful here," I said; "she could be pointing grouse." The season on grouse had been closed for a week or two.

Clover was locked up near a tangle of grapevines climbing on dead elms, and my assessment of the situation was right on the button.

"Thunk! Thunk! Thunk!" The wings of a ruffed grouse beat against the air and two others followed in close succession.

We both stood there with shotguns halfway to our shoulders, thumbs on safeties and fingers on triggers. But we did not fire.

I never took Clover or Pokey to the hill (grouse) country of southern Indiana during the early fall months because I did not want to tangle with either rattlesnakes or copperheads. But when the grouse season was extended through all of December and January Clover and I started having our fun.

Clover never liked to retrieve grouse—maybe because her mouth was so small she had trouble picking them up. But she was so cautious and would lock up on them at such great distances that I often would lose her on point for ten to fifteen minutes or more. When I would find her and let her know I was coming she would be as steady as a rock. When I would finally walk up behind her she would pussyfoot it through the brush until the grouse went up. I often would have to give the birds a chance to get away a bit before shooting to avoid shooting them up.

Just as Clover inherited Pokey's place in the house and in the field with me, she also assumed command of the passenger's side of the front seat of our car when we did not have another hunter with us.

She often would snooze at my side—her head close enough that I could scratch her ears—but if she was not inclined to sleep on those long drives to and from southern

Indiana, she would sit next to me, just as close as she could get.

However, sitting in this manner would sate her need for attention for only so long. After a short time she would turn, put her nose under my elbow, and raise her head sharply until she could raise my arm and slide under it to get even closer to me. She did this in the big chair at home, too, or anyplace else we happened to be sitting if she wanted more attention than she was getting.

Clover had a penchant for eating socks.

When Nancy would be sorting the kids' clothing before putting it away on wash day, she often would tell me one of the kids' socks was missing. After some observations of the back yard it was easy to conclude that Clover was eating them. The kids, naturally, would never wear them again, even though some came through, so to speak, without damage.

One time on the last day of the bird season in the middle of a cold and blizzardy day, Jim Ramsey had accompanied us to the Monroe Reservoir area. It was not a fit day to do anything outdoors—low temperatures, swirling snow, just a plain miserable day.

It was our last shot at bird hunting for the year, though, and we had been at it—with little success—since early in the morning.

Late in the afternoon Clover was crossing in front of us to go into the edge of a thicket and stopped long enough to regurgitate a knee-length red wool sock.

"Well, I'll be damned!" I told Ramsey as we inspected the sock. "I thought she was a little sluggish all day. Now I know why."

If Clover had a low point in her career it came in the wee hours of a morning when Ramsey and I had driven to Monroe to hunt ducks and birds with Tom Weddle.

I had told Tom the night before in a telephone conversation that we would fetch a box of donuts with us so he would not have to do anything but make a pot of coffee.

We got the donuts all right. But we made the mistake of leaving them on the front seat of the car when we went into Weddle's kitchen.

Since Ramsey was with me, Clover had ridden down in the back seat of my old Jeep wagon.

We had been in the kitchen less than a minute when Ramsey went charging back for the donuts. He came back carrying the mutilated donut box and said Clover was sitting on the passenger side of the front seat licking her chops.

One day as this chapter was being written Patty and Joan were reading from the computer screen over my shoulder.

"How do you remember all of those things about Pokey and Clover?" one of them asked.

I didn't answer immediately but looked, instead, straight out the den window past the two old leather collars hanging on the window frame above my desk.

"The remembering comes easy," I said after a lengthy pause. "It's the forgetting that is difficult."

At that moment I learned why there are times when a man cannot look his children in their eyes.

My Dual-Purpose Retriever

FOR TWENTY MINUTES or more I had stalked a flock of wood ducks while jump-shooting alone on Salt Creek upstream from Monroe Reservoir. When they flushed, two shots brought down two ducks.

That's when my problem started.

The first bird dropped close to the bank I had been walking, so I quickly leaned the little shotgun against a maple tree and slid down the bank to the edge of the water. With a strong dead limb eight or ten feet long I raked out the floating bird.

Retrieving that bird was no problem, but the other duck had dropped another fifteen yards downstream and close to the far bank. To make matters worse, it was drifting toward a large, windfallen maple tree—the banks of most

Indiana streams are bordered by trees—upon which a lot of driftwood had collected. To further compound my agony, the water was very deep and very cold, even though it had been an unseasonably warm fall and winter.

Would I go home with my limit of woodies? That was the question I asked myself as the second duck floated into the driftwood and stopped.

How would I get that duck? I could walk out on the trunk of the maple and straddle a large limb to scoot out within five or six feet of the duck. But then what? I would be closer—but still not able to reach the duck.

For several seconds I pondered that question while it got darker and darker on a cloudy day. Then it hit me like a bolt of lightning. There was a spinning outfit in the back of my Jeep Wagoneer less than a quarter of a mile across the field. If I remembered correctly, the last artificial lure I had tied on a month or so before was a six-inch artificial worm with three fair-sized hooks.

"It might work . . . it has to work," I told myself, heading back to the car at a brisk pace. Once there I grabbed the spinning rod and headed back on the run.

Why I didn't take off the shooting vest I wore over the old wool jacket I do not know, but I walked out on the tree trunk just as planned and straddled the big limb to scoot out the rest of the way. It wasn't easy scooting out on the limb while holding the spinning outfit. But I made it, and there was my duck—but a little farther away than anticipated.

I went right to work. By stripping line off the reel until the worm dropped down almost to the water, I could swing the lure like a pendulum and hopefully drop it just behind the duck. Then by raising the worm up and down slowly in the water, sooner or later one of the three hooks would stick in a wing, or better yet a leg, and I could fetch in the bird.

As the old saw goes, however, the best-laid plans of mice and men can still go awry. If one tried to pull a lure with three hooks over a log, all three would hook something. Not so with the duck. Several times I had the line seesawing on the side of the duck, but each time the lure flipped over and I had to swing the lure out again.

Then it happened. I had dropped the worm just behind the duck and was starting to raise it when suddenly there was a tug on the rod tip and the line was nowhere near the duck. By the time I realized what had happened, a fat crappie had taken my lure back under the driftwood.

I coaxed the fish out, however, and placed it in the game bag of my shooting vest. Another nice crappie and a keeper bass followed in quick succession before the duck finally was hooked, and as I scooted and walked back to the bank on the tree I was thumped on the back by all three fish.

As I drove home that night my mind ran rampant on my newly found retriever, and I started looking for telescoping spinning rods the next day.

Now, when the subject of jump-shooting ducks comes up, I can hardly wait for somebody to ask: "How do you get 'em, once you knock 'em down?"

Frankly, I think it is nice to have a retriever that does not require expensive dogfood for sustenance, nor chew up the furniture. To be brutally frank—some folks I know call it crude—I find it invigorating, perhaps even a tad Spartan, to skinny dip for downed ducks when my collapsible fishing tackle fails.

I realize, of course, that this can be dangerous because the human body probably should not be exposed (if you will excuse my choice of words) to ice-cold water in the dead of winter.

However, when the occasion arises in which I figure to

either lose a downed bird or take a dip, the folks who think I am all wet have hit the nail on the head.

Skinny dipping for ducks is not a new thing with me. My first experience at this sort of thing occurred on a fall day when I was a junior in high school at good ol' Crothersville.

Members of my high school class had ordered class rings soon after our junior year started. The idea was, I think, that the rings would arrive the following spring and we would have them on our fingers when our senior year in high school started.

But the rings came late that fall, and the day after I received my ring I chanced to be "plinking little black squealers"—stalking wood ducks with a rifle—on the east fork of the Muscatatuck River with Jack Cain.

The idea was to get as close as you could with the ducks on the water and "plink" one or two in the head before they could get away. This kind of hunting, incidentally, probably has had a lot to do with my success at stalking ducks with a shotgun later in life. It is, of course, unlawful to shoot ducks with a rifle now.

Jack had killed a drake woodie, and it was close to the far bank of the widest and deepest hole in that stretch of the river. There wasn't much current because water levels were low at that time of year and getting that duck meant walking all the way to Slate Ford Bridge, a mile or more away. With the sun dropping fast, there was no time for that.

We didn't know what to do—we certainly did not want that duck to be wasted—and finally Jack said the magic words.

"You can have that duck, if you'll swim out there to get it," he said.

The water was very dark and mysterious and that deep

hole always had put a little fright in my soul. But I peeled off my clothing, slid down the bank, and prepared for the worst. That duck could not be wasted.

"Toss your ring up here and let me hold it," Jack said. "The cold water might shrink your finger and you could lose it."

I hit the water like a thunderbolt and was a third of the way across the pool before I realized how cold it was. With Jack cheering me on, I grabbed the duck, turned and was on my way back.

Coming back was not so fast because I had grasped the duck's neck between the thumb and index finger of my right hand. With fear of cramps in my legs running through my mind, I made it.

When I was dressed again and picked up my little rifle, Jack handed me my ring. It was very loose on my finger, and I marveled at Jack's wisdom—without thinking of how stupid I had been.

Several years later I refined my skinny dipping methods on a November day on Salt Creek east of Monroe Reservoir.

This time I was hunting alone and the creek was probably four or five feet above normal level and muddy.

I knocked down a male woodie, which dropped at the middle of the creek. But the duck got into an eddy in the current before I could ready my retriever, which consisted of a collapsible spinning outfit with a surface lure attached.

I worked as fast as I could in getting the spinning gear ready, but the current took the bird back under some driftwood on the far bank. It was obvious that I would have to walk to the bridge and come back for my duck or get wet.

If swimming for Jack's duck was stupid, this attempt

was twice as bad. If I needed help on this one I would be up the proverbial creek without a paddle. Still, I went. I stripped it off and went, even though it was an overcast day dotted with occasional snowflakes.

But this time I got smart.

When I had thrashed across the swift current to reach the duck, I placed its neck in my mouth and came back full speed ahead, undoubtedly looking very much like a cross between Spitz (Mark, that is) and King Buck, the famous black Lab of Winchester's Nilo Farm.

I must confess that the woodie tasted better after I had baked it (stuffed with apple, onion and celery chunks).

Perhaps I should give up skinny dipping for ducks. It is not likely that the threat to life and limb will be any greater than it has been in the past, but I must admit the episodes are getting more complicated.

My last performance came during the early teal season a couple of years back. I was hunting a small, out-of-the-way private lake near Franklin with Colts player Ron Solt (now with Philadelphia) and Nick Banos, an educator who lives at Franklin.

We were souped in by a heavy fog when daylight came, but the sun burned that off in an hour or so and when a lone blue-wing came to investigate our decoys he was dropped without ceremony.

The wind was right to bring the bird to the shore, but aquatic weeds in the shallow water trapped it.

"I'll get him," I proclaimed, fishing my retriever from the five-gallon bucket I use for toting extra shells, cameras, binoculars, duck calls and sundry other accessories.

In less than a minute my retriever was rigged with a Ratta-lure (surface bait) and I shot a cast over said duck. I could see that Ron and Nick were impressed when my lure kissed the water only a foot or so behind the duck. There was only one problem. Somebody had tied a lousy clinch knot when he bent on the lure. As a result, the line did not go with the lure.

This turn of events set me to muttering that the lure out there on the water was the only one I had with me and that retrieval of that duck would require some skinny dipping. Off came my duds.

This one did not require swimming because the water turned out to be no more than knee-deep, but as I returned with the duck and my errant lure I suddenly realized the occasion was being duly recorded by Nick and his single-lens reflex.

"Sally Rand could have made a million with a blue-winged teal," Nick said in describing my efforts to hide.

Unfortunately, that was not the end of the episode. I now have to attend every Franklin Ducks Unlimited fund-raising banquet with a grocery sack of money for bidding on items I do not want because there is the constant threat that the picture will be enlarged and sold to the highest bidder at the first banquet I do not attend.

No! There's nothing wrong with wondering "how do I get 'em once I have knocked 'em down." But don't ask that question unless you are prepared to listen to a story or two.

Big Mitch and the Bullheads

NOT MANY HOOSIER ANGLERS who admit to being devotees of the catfish clan will admit they get much satisfaction from catching bullheads, but I learned on a late spring night many years ago that this member of the whiskers set can provide not only some exciting fishing but some excellent eating as well.

The year has long since escaped me, but this fishing adventure must have occurred in the mid-1930s and undoubtedly on an early May evening, because school had just ended.

I was privileged to be a junior member of a party which included my older brother, Jake; Garland (Big Mitch) Mitchell, a neighbor boy the same age as my brother; and Big Mitch's younger brother, Garnett, who was known as (you guessed it) Little Mitch. I was considerably younger than the others, and I probably was invited on this fishing trip because allowing me to go would make it easier for my brother to get permission to make the trip.

At any rate, the four of us spent a good part of the afternoon preparing lines for the trip and collecting bait.

It was to be a trip similar to many I would later take with my father to put out setlines baited with large sunfish, sucker minnows and other live bait fish to catch a flathead or blue catfish. This trip would be somewhat scaled down. The hooks and lines were smaller and so were the bait and the fish. We would use garden worms for bait and our quarry would be bullheads, the smallest member of the catfish family.

Our trip also would vary in that we would stay with our lines as long as the fish were hitting and we would run them every hour or so—more often if we thought it necessary.

Thus, when the sun started sinking on this beautiful spring day, we headed out across the fields with a lantern, a sack of sandwiches and apples and our bait and lines. Our destination was the Little Dredge Ditch, which started north of Crothersville, our hometown, and ran westward for two or three miles before turning south to feed into the Muscatatuck River in the vicinity of an area known as Twin Bridges. We would be fishing near a low-water bridge just below Pres Rider Hill. Just getting there was a rare experience for me because we were near only one road in going and coming and we only crossed it. The rest of the trip was through the woods and over little-used wagon trails.

I don't recall a lot about the trip either going or returning home. But I do remember that there was a large brier patch just below Pres Rider Hill and that for some reason my brother and Garnett walked around one side and Big Mitch and I went around the other.

We were about halfway down the side of the brier patch

when a big red fox burst into the open field just ahead of us and put on a dazzling display of speed, the large, bushy tail flowing out behind the smooth-gaited animal. The fox obviously had been spooked in our direction by my brother and Garnett.

Big Mitch, who was one of the finest and most talented athletes Crothersville High School ever produced, ramrodded this fishing venture, just as he did most of the other outdoor (hunting and fishing) trips we would take together. This, of course, would not have been a surprise to anybody who ever saw him blast a baseball into the apple orchard from either side of the plate, or run the high hurdles, put the shot, or play basketball. He was a natural-born take-charge guy.

Take, for example, an incident which occurred when Big Mitch and I had gone to Buck Ditch, half a mile north of Crothersville, to fish after a rain one afternoon.

True to the old saw about "the grass being greener on the other side of the fence," the fishing looked better on the other side of the creek.

Getting there would be no problem for Big Mitch because at the narrowest point the creek was only about six or seven feet wide and the banks were fairly high—at least a yard above the water. Moreover, the bank on which we stood was about a foot higher than the bank where we wanted to be.

Big Mitch would just back off, he said, and jump it—just as he would complete a broad jump in a track meet.

Getting me across the rain-swollen stream would be more of a problem, but Big Mitch came up with a solution.

He would simply sit me on the palm of his hand and shot-put me across the creek.

How he ever pulled it off I don't know, but once he had me sitting on his hand, he took a couple of shuffle steps toward the creek and his muscular right arm shot up and out like the arm of a catapult.

I went flying across the creek with arms and legs flailing the air and hit on the grassy bank on the far side. It was not a beautiful landing and it did not feel any better than it looked. Still, I was there. And when I had determined there was nothing broken, I got up and awaited Big Mitch's arrival. Of course, he made the jump with ease.

Now back to those bullheads.

Once at the Little Dredge Ditch that night, we picked a place that bordered a good hole of water and offered a nice flat bank where we could fish with hand poles by the light of a fire while waiting to run the set lines at intervals of forty-five minutes to an hour.

Then, as the night closed in, we combed the creek banks for several hundred yards each direction to position our set lines and bring back any driftwood we could find to feed the fire.

We had cut poles for fishing at the fire during the last part of our walk to the creek, and to each of these we attached a strong line about the same length as the pole. Our rigs were completed by tying one hook to the end of the line and a second hook on a dropper line a foot or so above the sinker. This rig puts one bait on the bottom— or very close to it—with a second bait only a few inches above the bottom.

When darkness came—the best time of the day for bullhead catfish—the fire was going good, and we each had brought in armloads of dried weeds from the previous growing season to fashion resting spots on the damp earth next to our poles.

The fishing was never real fast that night with our hand lines, perhaps because of the light of the fire. But now and then one of our poles, the butts of which had been jammed into the bank, would slap the water and the owner would jump up and yank out a bullhead. The fish ranged from five or six inches to almost a foot.

Often the lucky angler would jerk the fish out with such force that it would fly over his head—this is known as "Wabashing" a fish in southern Indiana parlance—and into the weeds and brush behind.

Our set lines were nothing more than miniature throw lines, each having an ounce or so of weight at the end of a strong line ten or fifteen feet long with four or five dropper hoods. The end of the line was tied to a willow or a root and the line was "thrown" out gently after swinging the weight like a pendulum in the direction it was to go. Tossing out a throw line, incidentally, requires a certain amount of skill, because the entire line must be held off the ground and kept untangled if it is to be a successful heave. It is somewhat like throwing a cast net, except for the fact that the cast net does not have hooks.

Running the lines was more exciting than watching our poles at the fire, probably because we never knew what we might have.

Highlight of the trip came when Big Mitch hauled in one of our lines to find a fat bullhead on each of the four hooks. Several other times he brought in two and three fish on a single line and we all went wild every time this happened.

The fish stopped biting—or at least the action became very slow—about 10:30 P.M. But by that time we had two big strings of fish, so we rolled up the lines and headed for home.

It was almost midnight by the time we got home, but that was not too late to awaken everyone at our respective homes to show off our fish. There were twenty-five bullheads on the two stringers and they tipped the scales to twelve pounds.

I was more an observer of the cleaning operation than

anything else, but Big and Little Mitch and my brother Jake made short work of the fish. When they were finished there was a good mess of catfish for each family.

The fish were fried for supper the next night at our respective homes and I must say that they were as good as any fish I had ever eaten. My grandmother rolled them in a mixture of cornmeal and flour and pan-fried them whole (heads, entrails and skin excluded) on the old wood-burning cookstove.

There were, of course, boiled dried beans, fried potatoes, cornbread and a few other side dishes which contributed to the success of the meal. But I learned right there that bullheads are worth considerably more as food than the salt you use in frying them.

I still enjoy fishing for bullheads the way we did it that night on Little Dredge Ditch, but since that time I have refined my fishing methods and the manner used by the two Mitches and my brother to clean our fish.

For example, I like to fish for bullheads during the daylight hours, too—especially after a spring rain has muddied up a small stream. Bullheads are primarily late afternoon and night feeders, but if a rain roils the water of a stream and causes it to rise this species cannot resist the temptation to go on the prowl for food.

A more important change comes in the method of cleaning bullheads. Many anglers I know still scald their bullheads with hot water and scrape off the slick skin as our fish were cleaned many years ago. But it is almost as easy to skin this fish with a sharp knife and a pair of pliers, and this method of removing the skin does not precook the meat.

I can't recall who said it, but one night many years ago while I was listening to a discussion by several old-timers on the "liars' bench" at Crothersville, one of the men was questioned as to why he liked bullheads so much on the table.

His exact words have escaped me, too, but the gist of his answer was that so far as bones are concerned, bullheads are about as close to the banana as you can get in whole fried fish.

That's good enough for me. The fried bullheads, I mean.

While Big Mitch, who is now retired and living in Florida, is on my mind, I would like to tell another story or two.

Once on an autumn day which had been blessed with a heavy fall of wet snow, we were roaming the woods west of Crothersville and grew wet and chilled at a place called Indian Hill.

This was a typical little beech-maple-hickory woods where rumor had it Indians once lived and we liked to go there because the sunken holes and mounds made it rather mysterious—like maybe Indians really had lived and been buried there.

At any rate, our clothing had gotten wet from the snow-covered brush. Since we were not moving a lot, we both were cold.

Big Mitch took care of that. He collected some dry twigs and soon had a roaring fire going. It was welcome.

The fire kept eating up the smaller dry sticks, however, and Big Mitch went after larger logs, coming back with a limb some eight or ten feet long and three to four inches in diameter.

He tried to break the limb several ways without success. Finally he grabbed it a couple of feet from one end and swung it like a gigantic baseball bat at a small tree near the fire.

That made two pieces of the limb all right. But the piece he was not holding came through the air like the blade of a helicopter—I still remember that "W-H-O-S-H, W-H-O-S-H, W-H-O-S-H" sound—and smacked me square in the kisser.

I awakened with a bloody snoot, lying on my old

sheepskin-lined coat in the snow, with Big Mitch (very worried) wondering how I was feeling.

Fortunately, the end of the limb which hit me was partially rotten and was softer than your run-of-the-mill tree limb. We soon were back in the business of exploring Indian Hill and I was little worse for the wear.

While Big Mitch was good at everything he did, he was really my guru (though that word had not yet been invented) when it came to making slingshots and other primitive weapons. He used them just as well as he made them.

Big Mitch would watch as ash saplings, which almost always have opposite limbs, developed forks in just the right size and angle, and when one was just right he would cut it for a "flipper" fork.

The Pennsylvania Railroad bed was made of beautiful rounded stones—many the size of marbles, but heavier—so we always had a ready supply of ammo.

On Sunday afternoons after church we would cruise the downtown alleys picking up empty whiskey bottles and tote them to a place north of town where the railroad tracks and the old Indiana Railway interurban tracks ran parallel some fifty yards apart. Since both were elevated twenty feet or so and there was a depression between the two, it was a perfect place to shoot slingshots at the bottles in the air.

We had constructed a small shelter in the depression where one person could stand, protected from falling glass and bottles. This person would fling the bottles straight up and a battery of shooters would try to break them. Little wonder that Big Mitch got very good at shooting a slingshot and that some of the rest of us became passing shots.

How good Big Mitch got with the slingshot is perfectly illustrated by an incident in the gravel-dirt road on the north side of the Mitchell home.

Big Mitch, who had turned a handful of horseshoe nails into finger rings (the nail heads served as the set, or decoration), gave me ten of the rings and had me toss them ten or twelve feet into the air.

He stood in a position that would send his projectiles out over a large field where the bark was skinned off utility poles and shot at the horseshoe nail rings as I tossed them up.

I tossed up ten of the rings. The exact number of hits escapes me now, but it was either six or seven.

Dabble Away the Day
or
A Close Encounter with a Bass

"IT'S NOT HOW FAR YOU CAST," my dad said. "It's where you put the bait (lure) that counts."

Having thrown out that bit of advice, he slipped quietly between two clumps of willows with intertwining branches and stood over a small pool of water on Grassy, a small creek north of Crothersville.

There weren't many people who knew Grassy hosted largemouth bass in both good numbers and size, and we didn't spread the word any more than necessary. But we fished it every time we had the chance and this was one of those days.

Two or three years before, my dad had bought me a South Bend No. 450 bait casting reel (which I still have) and a five-foot, solid-steel Gep casting rod to go with it. He put himself back into the bass-fishing business with a South Bend No. 550 reel and five-foot rod. Gradually we had acquired a collection of artificial lures which were not all that plentiful through the post-Depression days.

So it was that we were walking the banks of Grassy that day and my dad had seen fit to enlighten me, which he did occasionally, on one of the fine points of bass fishing—what he called "dabbling." Bass addicts today call this kind of fishing "flippin'" and I have heard a number of other names for it in the past. But to me it always will be dabbling, not to mention being one of my most interesting and productive fishing methods.

There wasn't much room when we both stood inside the tiny opening that overlooked the pool, which was no larger than a washtub. Willows and other brush surrounded the water and it was obvious even to my inexperienced eye that the greatest caster in the world could not put a lure into that spot, even though inch for inch it looked bassier than any other water we had seen on the creek.

"Watch," my dad said, stripping some loose line from his reel with his left hand while holding the rod handle in his right hand and thumbing the reel. He poked the tip of the rod with the Johnson Silver Minnow (dressed with Hawaiian Wiggler skirt turned backwards) through a hole in the willows and allowed the lure to pull about two feet of line through the tip guide as it hung suspended above the water.

A few seconds later he gave the lure a slight swinging motion with the rod tip. When it was swinging back and forth like a pendulum across the pool he released the line in his left hand at just the right time and the lure shot back under the willows on the far bank.

We watched the lure wobble toward the bottom as it sank in the clear water, and saw a two-poundish largemouth bass shoot from under the overhanging willows to nail the lure.

"See?" my dad said, as he set the hook and kept the bass coming right on out by thumbing the reel tightly and putting hard pressure on his rod.

Indeed, I did see. I saw so well that dabbling became one of my favorite methods of bass fishing. Of course, I have added some new wrinkles to the sport since the day my dad gave me my first lesson in this method of fishing, but the results don't change much. It is a great way to catch any fish that will take either a live or artificial bait, especially if the fish in question are hiding under heavy cover, or if there is not enough room to get the lure in the water with a conventional cast.

This should not surprise anyone. After all, nearly all game fish like good cover—especially during the bright hours of a sunshiny day—and dabbling will not only make it possible to get your lure into that kind of cover, but it will help you keep it there longer.

I dabble with just about any type of lure I may be using, but the jigs and spoon types probably are best suited to this kind of fishing because they can be fished straight up and down if this kind of maneuver is required. However, I use these tactics successfully when I am fishing a variety of plugs, spinner-bucktails and other types of lures.

I find dabbling most effective when I am wading a stream because fishing in this manner puts me very close to many forms of good cover. But dabbling can be used effectively any place the angler finds himself close to structure, whether it be on a river, lake or pond.

Take, for example, a day more than twenty years ago when I was fishing the newly opened Monroe Reservoir with

Tom Weddle while preparing a column on the bass-fishing virtues of the state's largest body of water.

Tom, then fish and wildlife manager of the reservoir, was giving me the "cook's tour" of the bass-infested reservoir in a twenty-foot jonboat and I was enjoying it immensely because I had the only copy of a lure called the Lutz Boomerang—at least the only copy of which I had ever known. Moreover, the Monroe bass were going crazy over this jiglike lure and I was working Weddle over pretty well. Nobody outfishes Tom Weddle with any degree of regularity, but I was doing it on this day from my perch in the front seat of the boat.

It was a sunny and windy early spring day and somehow Tom suddenly lost the ability to handle the boat. My end wound up back in some willows and brush so thick that I could not have shot my lure out of there with a cannon.

Thinking this was purely an accidental and temporary condition and with the realization that I could stand a little rest, I relaxed for a few minutes while Tom continued to whip the water to a rich, creamy lather with his ineffective casts, seemingly oblivious to my predicament.

When I was not extricated from this bear's nest in a reasonable period, I started a chain of throat clearings and other overt reactions aimed at letting Tom know I could not fish. Finally I declared in no uncertain terms that if I didn't get out of that bear's nest pretty soon somebody would be getting some bad press.

Tom laid it on the line with the declaration that he finally had me where that "damned contraption" (the Lutz Boomerang) could not catch a bass and that I might just be there for a spell.

At first I accepted my fate and started to relax some more. But then I noticed the bassy-looking water all around me—all those inundated willows—and my tendencies to dabble took over. I stripped a few feet of line off my reel and slipped the black-haired lure through an opening in the willows before allowing it to disappear into the greenish water no more than two feet from the bow of the boat.

When the lure touched bottom I took up the slack and gave the rod tip three or four twitches upward. You know the rest. A husky Monroe bass inhaled the lure. I set the hook with a vengeance and kept the bass coming right on into the boat with the same motion—just as my dad had done it many years before on Grassy.

With that one unhooked and flopping in the bottom of the boat, Weddle could see the writing on the willows and was trying to get me out of there pronto. That wasn't fast enough.

I went back after—and nailed—another bass, this one larger than the first.

That turn of events put Weddle on the oars again. Otherwise I might still have been there yanking bass out through holes in the willows.

On another occasion several years back, the Hoosier Outdoor Writers (HOW), Indiana's official group of outdoor writers and broadcasters, was staging its annual meeting at Salamonie Reservoir.

For several years Al Spiers, outdoor-environmental editor for Nixon Newspapers since the year after Indiana gained statehood (give or take a few decades), had been giving me the hard sell on Lake Michigan fishing because he lived and breathed it. I wasn't hard to sell, either, except for the fact that every time I went on the lake seasickness made me a basket case.

With Al coming to the HOW meeting, I figured my chance for revenge was at hand.

"Bring some old shoes, trousers and other stuff for wading," I told him on the phone. "When the meeting is over on Sunday afternoon we'll go wade one of my favorite little creeks for goggle-eyes."

Al came prepared—ultralight spinning gear and a grand assortment of miniature Lou Eppinger Dardevle spoons—and we motored to this stream, the name of which I just can't seem to remember.

Soon we both were catching rock bass like they were going out of style—not to mention an occasional smallmouth—and like the good host that I sometimes turn out to be, I fished slowly to give him first shot at the best spots.

After an hour or so he stopped midstream on a boulder-filled riffle and waited for me to catch up.

For several minutes we stood there discussing the joys of goggle-eye fishing, but before we decided to proceed with more of the same I asked if he had fished around the big rocks that flanked us.

"Yep!" he said. "Nothing here."

I couldn't believe there wouldn't be a redeye under the big rock at Al's side, so I stripped off two or three feet of line and dropped the sixteenth-ounce black Hairy Worm I was using almost at his feet. When it reached the bottom, I jigged it a couple of times and came out with a flouncing goggle-eye for the sack.

"You blankety-blank," he said, as he meandered off upstream again.

The story I am about to tell you is totally unrelated to dabbling, but the above mention of HOW brings to mind the formation of this organization more than twenty years ago, in 1969. You may find it worthwhile, at least for laughs.

When this group of outdoor writers met to organize,

one of the first bits of business was finding a suitable name. Our first thought was to name it the Indiana Outdoor Writers' Association, but we selected Hoosier Outdoor Writers instead, for certain acronymical considerations.

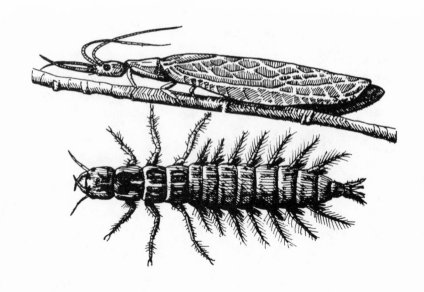

Throwin' Naturals

"WELL, NOW! If there isn't a smallmouth bass under that
log, I'll be mighty surprised," I told myself. There was nobody else to tell.

Lying half on my side and half on my belly, I squirmed
around to get a big yellow grasshopper out of the one-pound
Hills Bros coffee can which was suspended at my side by
a leather boot string tied (with slip knots) at both ends
of the can and looped around my neck.

I punched the point of the little wire fishhook through
one side of the big yellow hopper and out the other, then
pulled in the excess line with my left hand until the bait
dangled six inches below the tip of the little rod.

I eased the rod tip through a small hole in the brush,
being careful not to get the bait and line tangled, and when

all was ready I paid out the loose line with left hand until the hopper dropped lightly on the surface of the dark water.

The pool where I had deposited the hopper was no more than eighteen inches across, and most of it was completely covered by driftwood which had collected on the log. My head and shoulders were so close that I had to hold the little spinning rod out to my right side at about waist level.

At first nothing happened—the hopper just sat there motionless while the tiny rings it created lapped out gently at the log and other surrounding cover. After some time— probably only about a minute, although it seemed longer—I was just about to retrieve my bait and try something else.

About that time the hopper flounced a couple of times with kicks of those big jumping legs and that brought immediate action.

The surface of the little pool seemed to explode, and even though I had been prepared for this sort of thing, the fish still got the hopper and was gone under the log before I knew what was going on.

Lady Luck was on my side this time. When I got the smallmouth bass—a frisky twelve-incher—in close I grabbed the line to lift the fish through the brush in a shower of creek water.

My hopper was nowhere to be seen, but when I extracted the hook from the bronzeback's jaw, the hopper was in the fish's mouth. Being one who likes to use a bait until it is gone, I wormed the hopper's dead body onto the hook and brought the point out the tail. Then I fished a tiny split shot from my shirt pocket and crimped it on the line five or six inches above the bait.

I worked the rod tip back through the brush again—much as I had before—but this time when I paid out the loose line with my left hand the split shot took the bait right on down. But it didn't go far.

A sharp bounce of the rod tip ran up my arms like

so much electricity before the bait got to the bottom, and this time I set the hook more promptly to keep the culprit—a rock bass of seven or eight inches—coming right on out through the brush.

I tried my next bait on the surface without success, but when I rehooked it and allowed it to sink again beside the log it was gobbled up by another redeye.

Before the action cooled at this miniature spot I collected four rock bass to go with the smallmouth which later was freed to splash water on another angler. The rock bass would become part of a delicious fish dinner, and before I called it a day late in the afternoon there were more than twenty of them in the burlap bag which is known as the "Bayou Bill Creel" to some of my high-toned friends. Be that as it may, I know of nothing short of a live well on a boat that will keep fish in better shape, and not all live wells will do the job.

Making that live bait carrier mentioned above is a fast and simple operation. You will need a one-pound tin coffee can with plastic top, an old boot string or any other strong cord about four feet long and some sharp instrument for ventilating the can with small holes. I put the holes in the bottom of the can.

Just tie a slip knot noose at each end of the cord and loop both nooses around the can. Draw each noose tight and the can is ready to hold bait. The line will ride lightly on your shoulder, and you can adjust the cord to make the can hang at your side about any place you desire by simply shortening the cord with another knot or two or an extra half-hitch loop around the can.

I really prefer wide-mouthed mayonnaise jars with holes punched in the lids for my bait containers. I used them for several years. But fifteen or twenty years ago I slipped on a rock, hit on another and the mayonnaise jar shattered.

I was not injured in the flurry of unexpected action, but I did lose most of my bait. I have used coffee cans since that day.

My earliest recollections of fishing natural baits go far back to my childhood on the two forks of the Muscatatuck River that encircle my old hometown of Crothersville.

If you take the only blacktop road that leads west from this small community, you will pass the cemetery at what is now the west edge of town (it was half a mile out of town when I was a boy), and from there it is down over Burger Hill and into the floodplain of the river. The first bridge with any appreciable amount of water under it is the West (Vernon) Fork of the Muscatatuck River.

The old Muscatatuck has changed, as have most other streams and rivers of Indiana in the last forty or fifty years. But it still hosts a good population of largemouth bass and a number of other species, both game and trash fish.

When I was a kid the stretch upstream from the bridge was shallow on the east side with a clay-gravel-rock bottom and tapered off as one waded to the west side to three or four feet. The west bank of the river along this stretch was lined with water willow, which also grew in sizable patches anyplace else the current would allow it to gain a foothold.

To complete this angling classroom for poor boys who were not afraid to get their feet wet, the bottom of the swift water under and near the bridge was covered with large rocks (obviously left there by those who built the bridge) and hosted hellgrammites in good numbers through the warm months. And finally, along both banks of the river—especially in the area immediately up and downstream from the bridge—there grew a strange species of willow which I have found in only a few other parts of Indiana.

The hellgrammite is the larval stage of the dobsonfly.

It is difficult to describe either the hellgrammite or the dob-sonfly, but the best was to start is to say one is ugly and the other is uglier—and you can play vice versa with them any way that suits your fancy.

I cannot vouch for the value of the dobsonfly as fish bait. I haven't seen enough of these nocturnal critters in my lifetime to make such an appraisal. But when I think of hellgrammites as fish bait, I find it difficult to draw a comparison with any other bait, natural or artificial.

If I had to attempt a description of the hellgrammite, however, I would start by saying it is a black aquatic insect stage which ranges from a fraction of an inch to three or four inches in length, having a bodacious-looking pincer on its head. The leather-like body is segmented, and each segment along with the tail is blessed with rudimentary append-ages which fall far shy of being legs but which cling tena-ciously to rocks and other items, including one's fingers. The pincers of a large hellgrammite are not likely to mortally wound anyone, but I have had them draw blood from my fingers.

One of the best features of the hellgrammite's anatomy is the hard collar that covers the first segment of the body, just behind the head. By using light wire hooks, one can hook the mite under this collar, starting at the front edge of the collar on the back and bringing it out at the back edge. This will keep the bait alive. At times, it seems, the only way to kill one is to hit it with a stick.

Almost as strange as the mite I used for bait was the willow I used as a pole. This species of willow grew to heights of twenty feet or more, but I always selected a pole of eight to nine feet because this size range pole would be no more than the half an inch in diameter at the butt and would taper to the size of a match stem. These poles had an even softer action than the real fly rods, yet they were fairly straight until a fish was hooked; then they resembled a buggy whip. But that wasn't all bad for a kid who fished for fun as well as food.

The line consisted of everything from grocery twine or kite string to regular silk braids when they were available. But regardless of what was used, the rig worked best if the line was a few inches longer than the pole.

Long-shanked wire hooks—called sunfish hooks in those days—and wrap-on lead strips completed the tackle. When I wanted a bobber, it was usually nothing more than the cork stopper of a whiskey bottle (an easy item to find on Sunday mornings) with a slit in the side from top to bottom. Such a bobber could be slipped on and off the line with ease and would slide up and down the line to regulate depth. I still find such a bobber hard to beat.

The first order of business when I arrived at the river bridge was to catch bait. The hellgrammites would start getting scarce in late summer, but by that time there were hard craws—even some soft craws—under the rocks in the shallow water. There were also hordes of several species of grasshoppers swarming in the nearby fields. There was no shortage of natural baits at any time during the warm months.

With a hellgrammite hooked lightly under the collar or the white meat of a hard craw's tail impaled on the hook, I would wade the shallows to swing my offerings pendulum fashion quarterly upstream and allow them to drop in next to the beds of water willows.

A strip of lead wrapped around the line six inches above the hook would take the bait to the bottom, and there it would roll slowly downstream as I watched the line at the point where it entered the water.

When I would see the line stop or moving upstream, I would set the hook and the battle would be on. It didn't make much difference whether I had hooked a slab-sided longeared sunfish, a largemouth bass or some other species; with the willow pole it was always a fight.

One of the strangest natural bait fishing experiences I have been connected with came on the Blue River downstream from Fredericksburg a few years back.

I was floating and wading the Blue with basketball coach Bob Knight; Dick Lambert, owner of a canoe livery and bait shop at Fredericksburg; and Joe Ponder, a friend from nearby Palmyra.

We took a minnow seine along for catching hellgrammites and other baits the easy way.

The plan was to hit the best spots with artificial and live baits as we floated downstream. When we came to good riffles, we would tie the canoes to our waists and wade.

Joe was thirty yards or so downstream from a deep pocket where I was fishing when I heard him laughing.

"Come down here," he said. "You gotta see this to believe it."

Joe was holding a keeper goggle-eye in one hand and his fishing line about six inches above the hook with the other.

"I would like to say I caught this fish," he said, "but I didn't . . . my bait caught it."

There it was for the world to see. Joe's hook—still under the hard collar of the big hellgrammite, which was still very much alive—was nowhere near the mouth of the fish. But the ornery mite had grabbed the goggle-eye by the lip and would not turn loose.

Incidentally, using a minnow seine to catch hellgrammites is much more productive than trying to catch them with the hands, especially if there are at least two members of the party.

Just stretch the seine across a swift, shallow spot where

lots of loose rock, gravel or sand is found, then have some members of the party scrape around the gravel or sand and turn over the rocks with their feet. This action—called the hellgrammite dance by many natural bait anglers—will dislodge the mites, and the current will wash them into the seine. Hellgrammites, like other natural baits (including nymphal stages of many other aquatic insects) should be kept cool in a culture of damp leaves or weeds.

Still another fishing friend—Lewis (Lou) Bowsher—kept hellgrammites, crayfish and other natural baits in his thinning hair under a cap which fitted snugly around the sides of his head.

It is more difficult for a lone angler to catch hellgrammites and the larval stages of other insects which spend at least a part of their lives in the water, but I have been successful over the years by facing the current of a stream and turning large rocks over in such a manner as to have pressure of the current hold the mites against the underside of the rocks where they live. The hellgrammites are picked off the underside of the rock while it is under water by grasping them by the hard collar with thumb and index finger.

One of the greatest features of fishing naturals stems from the fact that getting the bait can be as much fun as the fishing.

Many years ago a Noblesville reader of my column told me about an experience he had with collecting bait back in the days when automobiles were the biggest thing since the invention of the wheel.

The name of the reader has long since escaped me, but his story will remain in my mind as long as it continues to function.

It seems that the reader—then a young man—and a fishing friend had gone on Saturday morning to a small creek, apparently south of Noblesville, to seine some minnows for a fishing trip scheduled for the afternoon. Although the day was hot and the sun was shining brightly, they were wearing hip boots, trousers and straw hats as they walked back to town.

Near the edge of town they noticed big yellow grasshoppers in good numbers in a roadside wheat stubble field and agreed that catching some of the hoppers might be a good investment of time.

Knowing that a minnow seine pulled through weeds will trap a lot more grasshoppers than they could catch with their hands, the two young men unfurled the seine and proceeded to drag it over the wheat stubble, much as they had when they were seining minnows.

While they were catching hoppers a motorist drove up the adjacent dirt road in one of those newfangled horseless carriages and saw the whole thing—two young men dressed for seining minnows but plying that ancient art in a stubble field.

Shaken by the sight of what obviously was two locos on a hot summer day, the motorist ran off the road and into a fence. Keeping a jaundiced eye on the two seiners, the motorist went into reverse to get back on the road and disappeared in a cloud of dust, still looking back over his shoulders.

One of my own personal bait collecting high points came back in the early 1950s when I worked for the American Can Company at Austin.

Jim Hall and Bob Bridgewater, two of my fellow workers, were joining me on a fishing trip one morning when we got off work at 6:00 A.M. The first order of business, we figured, should be seining a bucket of minnows.

I took them to this little creek no more than eight or ten feet wide and no more than three feet deep in most places. There was, however, a great little hole of water at one point—six or seven feet deep—and this figured in my plans.

Bob was carrying the minnow bucket and Jim and I were running the seine from our respective ends.

I was on one side of the creek and Jim was on the other. I told Jim that we would move against the current at a pretty good clip and that I would tell him when to cut across to my side to trap the minnows in the bag of the seine.

As we neared the deep hole I yelled, "Cut across, Jim!" His next step was his last. He was swimming and I was laughing out of control.

Of course Jim and Bob were great friends and I knew that I would get my just deserts in due time.

Justice did not dally. About noon my guard dropped ever so slightly as I bent over to check a reel at the edge of the lake and Jim and Bob hit me simultaneously from behind. I went in head first, but I had already had my fun.

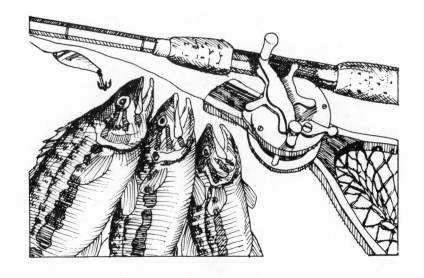

The Dragon Wins His Share

HUMBLE PIE has never been one of my favorite outdoor desserts, but I learned long ago that I must take the bitter with the sweet if I am to partake of the staples of nature.

I have been humbled by Mother Nature's children on a lot of occasions over the years, but the incident of this sort which stands out most vividly in my mind occurred more than thirty years ago, soon after I became outdoor editor of the *Indianapolis Star.*

It was a beautiful early October afternoon and I had one of my rare Saturdays off. Time, I thought, that my new bride, Nancy, should have a lesson in fishing for bass with live minnows.

I was well versed in the art of live minnow fishing, having studied under my father, one of the finest of the old masters of the Crothersville area.

So well, in fact, had I mastered the art of minnow fishing that while still in my early teens I had voluntarily—almost forcefully—given a lesson to one of the older men of the town.

On this particular day I was bankwalking, a name I gave as a boy to the practice of walking the banks while casting artificials to the best-looking spots for bass and other inhabitants of rivers and streams. There are times when I like to mix bankwalking with wading and floating. But if one sticks to bankwalking, he can cover a lot more river or stream, even though he will run into some waters that cannot be fished.

At any rate, I had enjoyed moderate success that afternoon on the east fork of the Muscatatuck River. I had two or three bass—all good keepers—in the mesh bag my dad had made for me, but time was running out when I came to the mouth of White Oak Ditch, which was a fine bass stream in its own right.

White Oak Ditch, which drained a long, bottomland basin from the east, created a deep hole at the point where it ran into the strong current of the river and there was a steep, straight-up-and-down bank on the upstream side of the river's east bank at the confluence of the two streams.

On the downstream side of the pool, however, there was a wonderfully flat bank which descended gradually to the edge of the water. If there was a better place to sit and fish with minnows or any other live bait, I had never seen it. Here one likely would find a largemouth or smallmouth bass if there was one about, and crappies seemed to like the steep bank just off the eddy created by the merging of water from the two streams.

The sun was below the tree line, and with the summer day coming to a close I figured to add another bass or two to my bag right there before trudging the two and a half miles into town. But my hopes for that died when I topped the high banks. There was Glen (Nig) Prince, one of Crothersville's best-known setline anglers, minnow fishing the mouth of the creek with two or three poles.

We exchanged greetings, and Glen's eyes told me he was impressed by the fish in my bag.

He asked what I had caught my fish on and I told him "artificials," shaking a Johnson Silver Minnow in the air as it dangled from the tip of my five-foot Gep solid steel rod.

As I sized up the situation, I had two choices. I could either horn in on his spot by fishing the outer fringes with my "store-bought" baits, or I could sit down and watch him fish with the hope that he would offer me a ride into town when he quit fishing, which I knew would not be long. I elected to watch and perhaps ride.

He told me his live minnows had produced several good runs, but he hadn't hooked a fish yet. Soon I knew why.

One of his bobbers sank and almost before it was out of sight he grabbed the pole and jerked it high over his head.

"Missed him again!" he said, and while I didn't want to appear a brash young whippersnapper, I knew why. I bit my tongue from my perch on a piece of driftwood and said nothing.

I must have walked in just as every bass in the river descended on the spot because before Glen could get that pole rebaited another bobber went down.

"Now let 'im go . . . give 'im some line," I yelled, not trying to upstage this older angler but eager to see him put a hook in that bass's jaw.

My frantic instructions came much too late. Glen jerked again like there would never be another chance and the bobber, bait et al. sailed over his head and landed on the bank amid a string of oaths which ended with something

like "I don't need a snot-nosed kid telling me how to catch
fish."

I thought about leaving right there. I really had no business telling this man how to go about catching a bass, but
the chance that I would have a ride to town at dark kept
my dust-filled fanny firm on that piece of driftwood.

When Glen missed another he must have seen the smirk
on my face and he could stand it no longer.

"If you're so damn smart, let's see you catch one!" he
said. "The hooks and sinkers are in my box, but I don't
have any extra bobbers."

I cut the artificial lure off my rod and placed it in the
little shoulder-strap bag I used for carrying such items. Then
I tied on one of Glen's hooks and wedged on a sinker.

The man who farmed the land had been using the shade
of some big trees on the high banks for resting his horses
at lunch time, and there were some corncobs there. I rammed
a strong, straight stick about the diameter of a pencil through
a two-inch piece of corncob. By throwing a couple of half
hitches around the stick on both sides of the piece of corncob,
I secured my homemade bobber to my line.

With one of Glen's fat and frisky minnows on the hook,
I cast to an eddy near the steep bank across the way. The
bobber was set to hold the minnow a yard or four feet
below the surface, and the current moved my bobber in
a little egg-shaped pattern about five or six feet long and
two or three feet wide.

Soon my bobber went down and Glen said something
to the effect that we would soon see how much I knew.

I was up for the occasion and soon was putting on the
same clinic my father had given me several years before.

"First you got to give 'em line," I said, holding the pistol
grip of my bait casting rod in my right hand and peeling
the braided silk line off the old South Bend No. 450 reel
with my left hand. "When a bass first takes a minnow it

usually is just holding the bait in its lips," I continued, trying to sound as convincing as my dad had sounded.

At the end of a short run everything stopped, but my corncob bobber did not return to the surface.

"There!" Glen said. "That bass has tangled your line in some brush and you'll lose hook and all."

"Maybe you're right," I said, "but I doubt it."

I continued my clinic by telling him the fish had just stopped to kill the minnow and turn it around so he could take it down head first. Pretty soon, I told him, the bass would swallow the minnow and take off again.

"When he does that, I'll sock the gaff to him," I said, getting a little cocky.

Sure enough, my line started moving again in a minute or two, and when the fish tightened up the slack I set the hook. After a short battle, I flipped the fish out on the smooth bank and jumped on it like a duck on a June bug.

"Well I'll be damned!" Glen said, adding in almost the same breath while ogling my bag of bass, "It's getting late . . . you want a ride into town?"

"Yep!" I said, adding that I would split my fish with him. Glen would have none of that: "You caught 'em, you keep 'em," he said. I could tell that he was not at all angry with me as his 1936 Ford rattled the planks of the old Slate Ford Bridge and we headed for town.

There would be many other opportunities to let my live-minnow fishing light shine in the future, and it always seemed to make me look like some kind of angling wizard.

Thus, as my bride without a trace of shame admitted to a marked lack of angling knowledge, I told her to fear not, that she would become an expert in no time under my tutelage.

We drove to the home of a farmer friend of mine on Big Brandywine Creek north of Shelbyville. After talking briefly with the farmer, we walked through the pasture to a deep hole on the creek where a gigantic oak tree had stood. The stump was all that remained.

That stump, a good five feet in diameter, was as flat as a tabletop. The water level of the creek came within a foot of the top of the stump, and I did not doubt that the earth had washed away from the roots below the surface, leaving a great place for many aquatic critters, including bass.

I jointed up the rods—a seven-foot spinning outfit for my wife and a nine-foot fly rod for myself—on the stream bank. Each had a hook, a small sinker and a bobber.

When I had baited the hook on her rod with a frisky minnow hooked through the tail, I handed it to her with instructions to step out on the stump softly (so she would not spook fish). When she was there, I told her to release the line by turning the reel handle backwards half a turn and allow her minnow to sink into the water until the bobber floated a few inches from the stump.

She followed instructions beautifully, but when the bobber came to rest on the water it did not stop. It kept on going.

"You got a bite already," I said, and intended to tell her to give the fish line. But I was far too late. She had started cranking the reel and when she felt the fish, she tried to yank it out. She got nothing, of course; not even the minnow.

"You gotta let 'em run," I started my spiel, just as I had told several other people. "Here, my rod's ready to go. Let me show you how."

With that I stepped out on the stump and lowered my minnow into the water at the edge of the stump, just as she had done. My bobber didn't sink immediately, but it hadn't been there long before the bobber quivered briefly, then dived.

I pointed to the bobber heading for the middle of the pool as I explained what was happening down there on the business end. Everything went just as I said it would. The bobber stopped—we could see it a foot or so below the surface of the clear water—and I had plenty of time to explain the wondrous, predictable workings of fishing for bass with minnow.

"There he goes again," I said with authority. "Now watch! When he tightens up the line, I'll sock the gaff to 'im."

Seconds later the bass tightened up the line and I set the hook with a vengeance, fully expecting to see my bamboo fly rod bend double and all hell break loose in that tranquil pool.

What I saw was a chub minnow and a sinker coming at me so fast that I didn't have time to duck. I don't know which hit where, but one hit me between the eyes and the other in the forehead.

Nancy tried to control her laughter, but she just couldn't handle it. I had made her day.

Later, while telling friends the story, Nancy said she laughed so hard she nearly fell off the stump.

She has never really known how close "nearly" was.

In the early years of our stay on Trail's End we bought a brand spanking new Ford Country Squire and camping gear to match because we wanted our children to grow up enjoying this sort of thing.

There was a nine-by-nine foot Sears umbrella tent, a collapsing picnic table with two collapsing stools, a Coleman two-mantle lantern, and a Coleman two-burner stove. We have since gone through a few tents, but we still use the old Sears tent occasionally and the lantern and stove are fixtures in our camping gear, although each has had at least one new generator as the years—going on thirty-five—have passed.

To get on with the story, the Division of Fish and Wildlife's put-and-take trout stocking program was just getting started at that time and I wanted to do a column or a feature to help push it along.

Folks at the DFW suggested that we fish Pigeon River in the area where it is joined by tiny Curtis Creek, so we headed that direction on a long weekend late in spring. The plan was to combine trout fishing with camping.

The trout stocked by the DFW that year were brookies, and while hatchery-raised trout do not sport the fire-engine-red bellies of natives, they were nice husky fish and I could see where we would have some fun.

Late on the second afternoon we went to the Pigeon at the point where Curtis Creek flows in. Somehow I got on the west side of Curtis Creek while Nancy was on the east.

Still having some purist blood in my veins at that time, I was using a fly rod. Nancy was using one of my favorite spinning outfits—a seven-foot Shakespeare glass rod with the action of a buggy whip and a closed-face Shakespeare spinning reel. She was using a miniature silver-painted Lazy Ike no more than an inch and a quarter long.

I was not doing much with flies, even though fish were rising, but she started doing land-office business with that little Lazy Ike.

I was ecstatic at the fact that she was doing so well.

"This ought to hook her on fishing," I thought—but I was somewhat disturbed that she was disregarding my instructions on landing the fish. Instead of winding them in until there was four or five feet of line still out and reaching down to lift them out of the water with her hand, she was winding them in within a few inches of the rod tip, then

"Wabashing" them with whatever backbone the rod may
have had. At times the rod appeared to be taking more
punishment than a pole vaulter's pole.

Tactfully, I told her several times that this sort of thing
could either break the rod, lose the fish or both. She agreed.
But the excitement of the next fish brought more of the
same, and this time my predictions rang true.

The weight of the fish did not break the rod, but the
fish—looking much like a bird—lost the hook in midair
and hit in the shallow water a foot from Nancy's feet.

She dropped the rod and pounced on the fish with both
hands and it squirted back over her head onto the level
bank, which was somewhat soggy from recent rains. Wheel-
ing around with the speed of a cat, Nancy grasped the trout
again with both hands and it squirted back over her head
again into the shallow water.

By this time I was so busy laughing that I didn't have
time to count the squirts, but eventually she accidentally
got a finger in the gills and came up with the fish. She
was mud and water from head to toe, but she nailed the
fish and held it up where I could see and simply said: "I
got 'im!"

At Crothersville they used to say "every dog has his
day," and I have always been a believer.

Some eleven or twelve years later—when Donna was six
or seven years old, as I recall—we were on a two-week camping and vacation trip to Ontario and Manitoba and had
flown into Barney Lamb's Ball Lake Lodge from Kenora
for a few days of fishing.

The walleye fishing was great, even though those one
and a half and two pounders far outnumbered the larger
fish. As a matter of fact, after the first two or three days
of fishing we still had not caught a five pounder.

Then the Indian guide took us to this surefire spot and

sure enough, Nancy got a hook into something that was really a brute.

With that same buggy-whip Shakespeare rod she used to catch the brookies at Pigeon River, she battled the thing for what had to be eight or ten minutes, and the way the fish was going—deep and powerful—the guide and the know-it-all outdoor editor concurred that it had to be a monster walleye.

"Hang on, Hon!" I kept encouraging Nancy, and at the same time refusing to take over the rod. Deep down I must have been hoping that it would break the line or escape in some other manner. One thing was certain: I would not be responsible for losing such a humongous walleye.

Up-and-down, up-and-down, the battle went. Each time she would get it almost to the surface in the dark water, it would dive to the bottom again and she would start all over. Each time I wondered why I couldn't get a hook into something like that.

Finally, though, she got it close enough for me to use the net and I made the sweep just in time. The hook came out as I pulled her catch into the boat.

Although the monster has now been relegated to a nice little niche under the basement stairway for several years, it still could be returned to its place on the living room hearth if need be—one twenty-and-a-half-inch, seven-pound four-ounce piece of genuine Canadian shale.

Uncle Harold, Uncle Remus
and Some Brookies

ONE OF THE GREAT JOYS of being outdoorsmen stems from the fact that we are in learning situations almost every time we go to the field and some good can come from almost everything we encounter.

"Is that right?" the TV interviewer (I think it was Channel 13's Don Hein) said. "Give me an example."

Taken somewhat aback by his request, I said: "Let's just suppose that I am walking in the woods and my path is blocked by a log. I step over the log and when my foot comes down on the other side, I am bitten on the ankle by a rattlesnake."

"That's great," the interviewer says. "But what did you learn and what earthly good can come from being bitten by a rattlesnake?"

"I just learned that one never knows what kind of critter might be lurking on the other side of a log in the woods," quoth I. "Being bitten by the snake made such an impression on me that I resolved on the very next New Year's Eve never again to step over a log without first looking to see what is on the other side."

To be honest about the whole affair, I have never been bitten by a rattlesnake. I have been gnawed upon by snapping turtles, bullhead catfish, squirrels, raccoons, and a menagerie of insects, including mosquitoes, no-seeums, deerflies . . . yes, indeed, deerflies . . . God bless 'em.

I can't remember the year—in the late 1970s, I believe. Our family was vacationing with my wife's aunt and uncle, Edith and Harold Smith at their cottage on Rondaxe Lake near Old Forge in upstate New York.

Harold introduced me to fishing for native brook trout on the Independence River and some of its smaller tributaries less than a year after Nancy and I were married. We spent a week or so with them every time we had the chance.

Apparently the word had filtered down through the family that Nancy had married some guy who was an outdoor writer. Harold (who for nearly half a century before his death in 1985 kept the Rome firefighting equipment in good shape when they could pry him away from his camp) couldn't wait to get a look at this city boy.

We went to Maine on our honeymoon after being married early in September 1954 (the fishin' was lousy because of a series of hurricanes), but the stage was set for an appearance at the Smiths' camp, along with a goodly number of other relatives, the following July.

Taking turns at the wheel, we drove straight through— something like twenty-three hours on those old-fashioned, two-lane roads—arriving at camp at 3:00 A.M.

Harold had been busy wrapping up loose ends at the fire station, so he had not yet arrived. I was able to sleep in that morning. But when Harold did arrive about 1:00

P.M., we all sat down in the camp's big dining-living room for a short talk. And when I say short, I mean it.

When the first silent seconds indicated that it was appropriate—less than fifteen minutes after Harold's arrival—he looked across the room at me and said, "Want to go fishin'?" Of course, we both did.

Harold looked my gear over out by his old Jeep and could find no fault with the little eight-foot Heddon bamboo fly rod, which heretofore had been used for bluegill fishing with poppin' bugs and rubber spiders, nor with my chest-high waders.

"I've got an extra creel [a beautiful old basket-like affair made of reeds]," he mumbled around the side of his pipe stem. When he fetched the creel he also handed me a crescent-shaped box for night crawlers and checked out his fly book to make sure he had a good supply of the nymphs which would be our first offerings.

"I only have one landing net," he said, "so we'll just have to make do."

"I won't need one," I said, and his lips seemed to part with one of those "Oh! won't you?" smiles.

Harold, who several years earlier had undergone surgery that would have stopped a moose and still must have suffered immeasurably with his malady, nursed the old Jeep over some fourteen miles of mountain logging roads, around boulders nearly as large as the Jeep itself, through marshy areas, around downed trees and across "bridges" which amounted to no more than two parallel plants. Finally there it was, the Independence River.

"We're here at just about the right time," Harold said, hastily jointing up his fly rod and bending on a little gray nymph. "If they don't take flies right away, we'll switch to worms. We don't have a lot of time."

The trout did not hit flies that afternoon. But when we came to a large pool in a bend of the river—one that Harold said would "float your hat"—he pulled out a pair of nail clippers, cut off the fly and tied on a smallish hook (a short-shanked affair with a gap of about a quarter of an inch). He added a tiny split shot six or eight inches above the hook, which he baited with a half-inch piece of night crawler.

I rigged my outfit in the same manner, but before I could get into action Harold had caught two or three brookies in the eight to ten-inch class, gracefully scooping up each fish with his landing net and placing it in his creel. I attached no significance to it at the time but noticed that he did not take a fish out of the net until he had his finger in its mouth.

Before long I had a bite, too, and when I thought the fish had the bait in its mouth, I set the hook. The little rod arched and I played a dandy brookie to a standstill before reaching down to pluck it out of the water with my bare hand.

By the time I had succeeded in dislodging the hook from the brookie's lip, I figured that Harold, who was watching the episode, had learned that a big city boy could make do without a landing net. What I did not figure on was the next flounce of that brookie.

It came with the speed of light and the ease of falling off a log backwards when you are crossing a creek. In that split second the red-bellied critter was airborne and in the bat of an eye, PLUNK! He was gone.

Harold became very busy making a cast about that time, but I didn't have to see his face to know there was a smile there. My luck didn't change much in the next few minutes. Trout either flipped off the hook as I struggled to pick them up on the surface, or slipped out of my grasp before I could unhook them and get them in the creel. A wet brookie, you know, is more slippery than a bar of soap in the shower when you have both eyes full of suds.

Finally, though, I devised a plan that would have made

even Uncle Remus, Joel Chandler Harris's original "it's-what-you-do-with-what-you-got man," very proud.

I felt a fish take the bait, set the hook at just the right time and let out a war whoop to be certain Harold knew I had on a good one. I played the fish carefully until it was directly in front of my body (waist deep in the black water), then lifted the rod tip to gently flip the fish into the air. As it bounced off my chest, I pulled the front of my waders out with my left hand and literally trapped the fish in the old breadbasket.

When the fish was unhooked (still inside my waders), I slipped my thumb into its mouth, grasped the lower lip firmly and placed it in the creel.

I could not see Harold's face, but I was certain he was smiling at that turn of events, too, because I could tell he wanted me to succeed. Harold Smith was that kind of man —a lot like Uncle Remus.

In the years that followed—we tried to make it to the Smiths' camp only every other year to keep from treading on the welcome mat too often—Harold took me to favored stretches of a number of the streams in the Old Forge area.

On some occasions we would travel by boat before striking out through the woods, but mostly we would go by Jeep. No matter how we traveled we always came to a good brook trout stream, and to make the fishing even more exciting, they were almost always native fish. Now and again we would take a trout that appeared to have been hatchery stock, but not often.

If today someone should offer me the chance to return to any one of those stretches of water for an afternoon of fishing, I would drive straight through to get there. Still, there is that stretch on the Independence (where Harold took me that first afternoon we fished together) that stands out in my mind as the classic native brookie stream.

True, even as this piece is pecked out on my home computer, my eyes turn occasionally to the seven-pound, two-ounce native brookie I took on a wild river in the Northwest Territories. I often think of the trophy fish we took there. Still, when I laze in the big chair in the living room and liken the pink glow of a wood fire through the window of the little wood-burning stove to that of a cold sun sinking through the trees to the west, thoughts of native brookies come easy. They almost always are the seven to ten-inchers from the Independence. It is that kind of stream.

One afternoon when Harold Jeeped us into the Independence the fishing was very slow. We couldn't seem to catch any brookies at all—not even on pieces of night crawlers. They just didn't seem to be hitting.

We both had fished upstream from the spot where Harold had parked the Jeep and it seemed as though we lost all track of time. At least I did.

"We'd better start back to the Jeep," Harold finally said, looking to the west where the sun had disappeared behind heavily forested ridges some time before. "We have to be pretty well out of here before dark."

He didn't want to be driving over fourteen miles of abandoned logging roads after dark, especially when he remembered the boulders nearly as big as the Jeep we had encountered on the way in.

With that, Harold headed back downstream, fishing the best holes as he went.

Not wanting to crowd Harold as he fished, I waited a few minutes, then started fishing back downstream.

With the fish snubbing even pieces of night crawlers, I figured I might as well go back to flies and stopped long enough to tie on a little gray nymph, usually a killer on brookies on the Independence.

This didn't work either for a time, but when I cast the

nymph into the middle of a wide spot in the river—obviously a deep hole—there was immediate action.

Another cast produced another fish—beautiful fire-engine-red belly and all. Soon I was oblivious to the fact that it was getting darker and darker as I closed in on my daily limit of ten fish.

Soon I could hear Harold hallooing to me—obviously from the Jeep—and there was a sense of urgency in his voice.

But the trout were hitting so well and the spot was so beautiful in the gathering dusk that, as I later recalled, at one time the thought passed through my mind that if I were ever to see God, it would be right there. He would be sitting on the side of the overhanging mountain watching me fish.

When I had taken my tenth brookie, I thrashed through the brush as fast as I could to the Jeep, where Harold already had the engine running.

On the way out I told Harold about my thoughts on the beauty of the place where I was catching the trout and about the feeling of the presence of God.

"I hope He is sitting on these mountains, too," Harold said in that dry, upstate New York manner. "I could use a little help getting us out of here."

On another occasion—in the summer of 1975, as I recall—Harold had not been able to spend as much time at camp as he usually did when we were vacationing there because a rash of bad breakdowns in the Rome firefighting equipment was keeping him on the job.

He had managed to get up to camp on Sunday, though, and he left the Jeep there so I could get back in the boonies to the best trout fishing.

Before he left on Sunday evening Harold had explained and mapped for me, as best he could, the logging roads that would take me to our favorite stretches of the Independence, but lack of use and nature's constant fight to regain control of those mountains had taken their toll. The roads were no longer clearly defined at some spots.

I started to the Independence about noon the next day, but before I could find the river the sun was already dropping behind the mountains. I knew I did not have time to fish then. I would have to return the next day.

It had been five or six years since we had been at Edith and Harold's camp, and I wondered throughout the afternoon if the brook trout fishing would be as good there then as it had been almost twenty years earlier to the day when Harold had taken me there for the first time.

That night I told Edith and Nancy about having so much trouble finding the river and about my thoughts on the matter. Could it be as good now as it had been when Harold first took me there?

They, of course, had no idea.

I left at noon again the next day—I didn't want to fish through the hot part of the day. This time I had no trouble at all finding the place.

The first two or three pools upstream from the Jeep didn't produce much, but at "God's Pool" the action picked up and through the remainder of the day I kept only extraordinary fish or those I had reason to believe might have been injured.

I figured that would be plenty for the pan back at camp.

It was well past dark when I pulled back into camp and walked in the back door with my fish.

"Was it as good as twenty years ago?" Edith asked.

"Nope!" I said emphatically. "It was better!"

Now back to those deerflies.

I know you think this wandering old mind forgot the deerflies after making such a fuss of them earlier in this chapter. However, one—even an ancient one with a head like a house cat—does not forget such evil critters as deerflies when they are connected with an outstanding adventure with native brookies on the Independence River.

It was our last trip to the Smiths' camp. I had a strange "gut" feeling that it would be, and for the same reason I feared it might also be the last time I would get to fish with Harold.

The fire equipment at Rome was acting up something miserable, and though we did manage an afternoon on the Moose River near camp and up a nameless little creek filled with delightful little pools above and below the beaver dams, we would not make it to the Independence together.

To further complicate things, Harold's old Jeep was not working well. He didn't even have it at camp.

Through most of the week I fished the Moose and some of its feeder streams. I had a lot of fun. But when you have a long relationship with a brook trout stream like the Independence and you are within a few miles of your old haunts, you have this gnawing urge to go there, and it will not leave until you go. It is much akin to Kipling's explorer in the poem of the same name. (Incidentally, if you haven't read "The Explorer," you should do so at your earliest convenience).

Thus, on Thursday evening—with the last day of our camp stay coming up—I eased into the after-dinner conversation the fact that I had not been to the Independence yet and would like to try to make it there with our Jeep Wagoneer. I had no intention of taking it all the way over those old logging roads, but if it would get me within two or three miles I could hoof it in from there and have what I figured would be my last fling on this beautiful river.

"We [meaning the girls] want to go into the Forge shopping tomorrow," Nancy said. "We'll need the car."

I countered that she could run me up the roads as far

as possible and drop me off late in the morning. Then she could come back to pick me up about dark.

That's the way it worked out. Our Wagoneer got me within about three miles of the Independence, and I figured a hike of that distance would be a small price to pay for an afternoon of fishing for native brookies on a stream I might never again see. When I slammed the Jeep door and waved Nancy off I couldn't believe how smoothly it had all gone. My smile must have looked like an ultraripe watermelon which splits from one side to the other when you touch it with the point of a butcher knife.

It went smoothly, that is, until I watched the Jeep disappear around a slight bend in the road, leaving me alone. About that time I became aware of an unusually large number of deerflies, and when I walked into the first patch of shade I was met by a whining horde of mosquitoes, which were bent on eating me alive.

When I reached for the can of insect spray in my little shoulder-strap tackle bag, I had this strange feeling that I had not picked it up from the floorboard of the back seat of the Jeep when I grabbed my other gear. I was painfully right.

At that moment I knew I would have a fight on my hands. In the Adirondacks the skeeters can torment you unmercifully in the shade and the deerflies can eat you alive in the sun. But I was there until dark—there could be no doubts on that score. And I would fish, I told myself, if it killed me.

I remembered a number of occasions when I had returned from the Canadian bush covered with infected blackfly bites that made me look like a leper. Still, I knew I had to fish—insect repellent or no insect repellent.

About an hour later I arrived at the old wood bridge and jointed up the little three-piece Heddon bamboo rod that I had reserved for fishing native brookies for more than twenty-five years. It just didn't seem right to use the rod anyplace else. It seemed to be made for the Independence and those trout with fire-engine-red bellies.

With the rod rigged, I quickly changed from walking to wading shoes and started up the river, fighting the mosquitoes when I was in the shade and the deerflies when I wasn't.

I fished slowly and I fished as well as I could while waging a constant war against my tormentors. But the brookies weren't in the mood for the little gray nymph that Harold taught me to use the first time we fished this water. When the sun was getting close to the treetops on the ridge to the west I had only one trout in the old wicker creel.

By this time I was at the foot of the millpond pool and I figured this would be the place to start if I were to do much business on this day. Underbrush around the edge of the pond, which is a good seventy yards wide, kept the length of my casts down, and I did not score there either. But when I waded knee-deep into the fast, brown water where the river drops into the millpond pool, I thought conditions would be better. I could quarter the current with my casts here to make more room for back casts. I could cast considerably farther.

Here I was in the open, too, and this meant my war was strictly with the deerflies. Unfortunately, they seemed to be worse here than they had been anyplace else. They were so bad, in fact, that I was brushing them off my face and neck almost constantly, but I still managed to cast the gray nymph and work it as deep and as well as I could.

If there is anything nice to be said about deerflies it would have to revolve around the fact that one almost always can feel them when they sit down on bare skin. For this reason, it is possible to either squash them with a slapping motion of the hand or pinch them between the thumb and index finger before they have a chance to bite.

So it was that I was fighting a valiant battle with these critters even if I wasn't catching any trout.

Then the miracle occurred. A nice trout came to the surface within easy casting distance, and I picked up the nymph from its resting spot and delivered it to the spot where I had seen the fish. No need to go deep now—that fish was on the surface.

The little fly settled into the water nicely, but there were no immediate takers. While I waited another fish showed even closer to the spot where I stood. As I made a couple of false casts to try that one, another fish slurped something on the surface closer to the spot where my nymph had just been.

For several minutes I had trout rising at several spots, but they all had one thing in common. They were directly below me . . . in the current.

Again I cast to a rising fish—this one no more than ten or twelve feet away—and this time the fish slurped in the fly almost as soon as it had settled onto the water. I managed to land the fish and there I got lucky. As I unhooked it, the trout regurgitated—of all things—a fresh deerfly.

"Well, well!" I said. "I've been pickin' a smorgasbord for you picayunish little nuts. If you want deerflies, you'll get 'em."

Standing in my tracks, I started pulling deer flies off my skin and punching them onto the hook of the little nymph. When a fish would rise, I would serve up his dinner. Before long I had to stop and count my fish to avoid going over the limit.

That night, while sitting on the boat dock at camp and watching a shimmering swath of moonlight bisect the reflection of Bottle and Cork Mountain in the quiet water, I realized that my real accomplishment that afternoon had amounted to much, much more than merely catching a limit of brookies. The real accomplishment had come in reading the conditions and turning adversity into a triumph of sorts.

I figured a brace of uncles—Remus *and* Harold—would be proud of me.

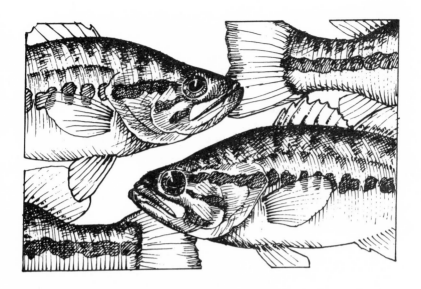

The Monroe Reservoir Bass Story

"SEEING IS BELIEVING," according to the old saw.

For this reason, it would be difficult to tell me a seemingly far-fetched story about bass fishing on Lake Monroe—Indiana's largest "inland" lake—that I would not believe. You see, I saw it. Firsthand, unadulterated, unabridged and almost unbelievable at times.

But like thousands—perhaps even hundreds of thousands—of Hoosier anglers, I had the rare privilege of seeing the bass fishery of the Monroe Reservoir develop. And of fishing this fifteen-mile-long body of water when it was hotter than a fire truck. Otherwise I might not have believed it.

To fully understand how good the bass fishing was at Monroe Reservoir in its heyday, one must also know why it happened. That, in itself, is a story.

Woodrow (Woody) Fleming, who still lives on a farm which borders Driftwood River north of Columbus, was director of the Division of Fish and Wildlife when Lake Monroe was constructed on the three forks of Salt Creek by the U.S. Army Corps of Engineers as the state's first multipurpose reservoir. Some other reservoirs had been constructed, but this one was touted from the start as multipurpose, not just for flood control.

Fleming and his staff were charged with the responsibility of stocking the 10,780-acre reservoir, not to mention providing a lot of input on physical features of the floodplain which would be retained. Long before the time came to stock the reservoir, the state agency determined that 1,400 adult largemouth bass—fish from ten inches up to five or six pounds— would be all they needed. This, of course, did not include the other species involved.

Thus, when the reservoir was impounded in the fall of 1964, most of the largemouth bass were placed in a pool of some 3,500 surface acres of water just above the dam. When this pool reached about 4,500 acres it was stabilized for the winter.

The reservoir filled slowly—the water level did not reach the pool stage of 538 feet above sea level until late the following year—but as the water crept slowly into the valleys up the three forks of Salt Creek to inundate agricultural fields, weed patches, thickets and a variety of other lands, those adult bass had all the food they could want. As a result, they were in great physical condition when the urge to spawn came in the spring and early summer of 1964. Spawn they did.

To further enhance the chances of game fish, all of the waters of the Monroe Reservoir watershed were killed out with rotenone to eliminate competition for the new residents from carp and other rough fish.

When the eggs of bass started hatching early in June

1965, biologists were astounded to find huge swarms of largemouth bass fry everywhere in the shallow water.

"It didn't make much difference where you went," Fleming said later in the summer, "there were swarms upon swarms of largemouth fry."

This first nesting success of the adult bass alone amounted to something of a lake-stocking coup in Indiana. Never before had our fish and wildlife agency produced anything close to it.

The fry quickly turned to fingerlings, and as they spread through the weed patches, over the flooded fields which had been planted to a wide variety of crops, and the woods, the growth rate was phenomenal. A great percentage of the fry produced the previous spring were more than six inches in length and some topped the ten-inch mark as they went into their first winter.

So great was the growth rate, in fact, that many of the bass hatched in the spring and early summer of 1965 spawned in the following spring and the growth rate continued. By the time the second spawning season had passed, it was becoming increasingly obvious that a bass-fishing bonanza was in the offing.

The reservoir had been off limits to all angling since the fall of 1964, when it was first stocked. That made two spawning seasons and three growing seasons between the time Monroe was stocked and January 1, 1967, when it was opened to fishing. During that time about the only thing that showed a greater growth rate than the bass was the feather in the cap of the DFW.

The DFW also had stocked bluegills, crappies and several other species of fish—including the big cats—and they were doing just as well in terms of growth rates as the bass.

Although the winter of 1966–67 was fairly cold, Monroe offered almost no ice when it was first opened to fishing.

Rank-and-file Indiana anglers were not accustomed to

fishing for bass during the cold months, but they knew the Monroe bass were there and they went after them the best way they knew—in boats with sturdy tackle and buckets of minnows.

Most anglers used bobbers to offer their minnows at various levels, but in a few days it became obvious to a few that the fish were right on the bottom. Off came the bobbers and on went the heavy sinkers—enough weight to take the minnows to the bottom—and up-and-down angling became a way of life with Hoosiers. It was different, this Monroe fishing, but it worked—and that was all that mattered.

For a few days the action was spread over the entire reservoir. But when the state's outdoor press started printing stories of success with great numbers of fat and husky bass on Sugar Creek Bay, the parade was on.

I didn't make it to Monroe until January 11. That was a day of fishing never to be forgotten.

To that point the fishing had been almost exclusively on open water because the winter had been mild and there was little or no ice. But the bottom dropped out of the thermometer the night before we were to fish Monroe, and when our two boats—twenty-foot flatbottoms with twenty-horsepower motors—left Fairfax ramp we started running into skim ice almost immediately.

Tom Weddle, the fish and wildlife manager for Monroe, was running the boat I was in, and we had been joined by his father-in-law, Albert (Red) Schafer. Two fisheries biologists were in the other boat.

Our boat broke a path through the ice for the other boat, but the closer we got to Sugar Creek Bay, the thicker became the ice. Soon Red and I were standing on either side of the bow of the boat breaking ice with the oars. This eventually failed, however, and it appeared that we would be unable to get to the hot fishing spots at the back of the bay. The ice was too thick to break but not thick enough to support a man.

Tom eventually had this brainstorm. He would back the boat up and unlock the motor so it would flip up when it hit the ice. Then he would run the bow of the boat up onto the ice and Red and I could jump out (with a firm hold on the gunnels of the boat) and mush it across the ice.

"If the ice breaks, fall back into the boat," Tom told us.

The plan worked to perfection. Soon we were closing in on the back end of Sugar Creek Bay, where the water was about eighteen feet deep and willow trees protruded.

Tom lined the boat up between three big willows where he had caught fish before the ice came and we were able to stand in the boat to beat holes in the ice with the oars.

I must admit that I had my doubts from the start about our chances for success on this day. But we hadn't much more than tightlined that first minnow to the bottom before it was coming back up with a fat and sassy Monroe bass. My doubts, needless to say, were quickly dispelled.

The two biologists in the other boat did not follow at first, but when they saw us hauling in bass they mushed their boat across the ice and moved in with us.

It would be impossible to guess how many bass the five of us caught that afternoon, but we each took in a six-fish limit and these bass ranged from fourteen or fifteen inches up to more than five pounds.

I had a new Pentax camera and recorded the whole thing—I thought. There was one small hitch. The film had not been advancing through the camera. By the time I made this discovery we were back at Fairfax ramp and it was much too dark to get decent pictures.

We did line up a bunch of bass on the pavement of the ramp and I tried to get pictures of them, but it was just too dark. All I got was outlines of one of the best strings of bass I have ever seen.

Monroe Reservoir had produced the best afternoon of bass fishing I had ever known. But the best was yet to come.

One day late in April of 1967, I returned to Monroe for a combination bass-fishing, morel-hunting trip with Tom Weddle. We started our trip shortly before noon on the bay on the left side of the road that now goes into Paynetown Recreation Area from the Visitor's Center on Indiana 446.

Weddle was showcasing the reservoir again for me—the Department of Natural Resources was proud of its coup and frequently rolled out the welcome mat for visiting scribes.

We were fishing in one of those twenty-foot flatbottom workboats, and the first thing I did was establish the ground rules.

"Let's get our limit of bass as soon as possible," I told Weddle. "I want to spend most of the afternoon hunting mushrooms."

It was about 11:30 A.M. when we started fishing for bass, and when I hauled in the first good keeper soon thereafter, I tied my burlap bag to the seat of the boat and tossed it into the water with the flopping fish in it.

In a workmanlike manner we went at the business of snaking in a two-man, twelve-fish limit of largemouth. I was keeping tabs on the fish as we placed them in the sack.

"That's number eleven," I said, unhooking a fish, placing it in the sack and allowing the sack to sink back into the water while noting after a quick look at my watch that it was not yet 1:00 P.M. "Let's get another one real fast and get after the mushrooms."

Here the plan hit a snag.

As the Bayou Bill creel went back into the water, I noticed

frayed edges in the side of the bag. I quickly told myself that burlap bags do not have frayed edges.

Upon lifting the bag into the boat I could see a hole in the side of the bag at least five or six inches wide, and the only bass there was the one I had just caught.

By way of explaining our problem to Weddle, while excusing myself for such a tactical error, I said the sack probably had been put away damp when I quit stream fishing the preceding fall and that the burlap had simply rotted.

"Oh, well," I philosophized, "there are more than eleven fish in this sea. Let's go get some mushrooms and catch another limit of bass just before dark."

Up the hollows from the edge of the reservoir at several points we came up with several bread bags of morels. We both were enjoying the mushrooming so much that we lost track of time. By the time we made it back to the boat on the last mushroom stop, the sun was down and darkness was coming on fast.

"We'll have to hurry if we're going to catch our limit of bass," Weddle said, cranking up the motor and heading for deeper water. But just as suddenly as he had started the motor, he cut it off.

"Look in there," he said, pointing to an inundated patch of weeds left over from the previous growing season. "Something's feeding in there and it could be bass."

With that Weddle tossed a jig-n-worm rig into the weeds and came out with a bass. I followed in rapid succession with a Johnson Silver Minnow dressed with a black and yellow Hawaiian Wiggler skirt.

We took our limits of flouncing, flopping bass right there and didn't bother to string them up until we were back at the ramp.

Z-Z-Z-Z-Z-Z-Z-Z-Z-Z-Z

THERE CAN BE no doubt about it—the explosion of a covey of quail over a good bird dog, the smashing strike of a largemouth bass on the surface late in the afternoon on a still day or any one of dozens of other experiences in the outdoors can be terribly exciting.

Yet there are times when I have these "tremendous ideas" about things to do, and when these times roll around everybody in my family knows that I am bound for a nap.

References to sleeping outdoors may be found in other chapters of this book for the simple reason that I like to take little catnaps—even full-blown snoozes—in the woods, on the creek bank, in stands of broom sedge, in abandoned barns and countless other places I have *not yet* tried. Those two words are emphasized for very good reason. I have a few years to go to run out the string.

The great Hoosier poet James Whitcomb Riley said it well in the opening verse of his poem "Knee-Deep In June":

Tell you what I like the best—
'Long about knee-deep in June,
'Bout the time strawberries melts
On the vine,—some afternoon
Like to jes' git out and rest,
And not work at nothin' else!

This habit of sleeping in the outdoors doubtlessly can be traced to my preteen and early teen days at Crothersville. It started soon after my dad turned me loose the summer I was ten years old to hunt and fish alone or with certain of the older men of the town.

I could take the little single-shot Springfield .22 bolt-action rifle out by myself or I could go with Jack Cain, John Peavler and a few of the other older men. But I dared not take the rifle out with kids my own age—or even other young fellows—because I knew my dad would live by his word.

"If I catch you taking that rifle out with other kids, I'll take it away from you," he told me. I knew the legislative branch of family government had acted. It was law.

Thus I hunted with Jack and the other older men as often as possible. They didn't always want to spend as much time in the woods as I did, and this helped me develop a loner streak which I still have—and enjoy. Hunting or fishing with other people can restrict or inhibit one's actions, but the lone outdoorsman can do as he pleases—and that pleases me.

For this reason, often during the squirrel season I would leave home well before daylight and not return until after dark.

I always had something to eat before I left home, and I always carried matches and a small container of salt. If

I couldn't find anything readily available to eat—say apples or tomatoes—I could always bake small fish or frogs (wrapped in damp sycamore leaves and caked with thick mud). Nor did young rabbits or squirrels go badly when roasted over a bed of coals.

In any event, a full tummy has spawned "tremendous ideas" in my mind since those wonderful years when I grew up on the Muscatatuck River and environs. I can at least hope this never will change.

Potable water also was one of my prime considerations in selecting places to take my naps, and as a result I could almost always be found during the hot part of the day flaked out in the shade near a spring or some other waterhole. Knowing the location of free-flowing springs and tile drains was every bit as important to me as keeping tab of which hickory trees were being cut heavily by squirrels. I can't remember ever becoming ill from drinking the water at riffles of the Muscatatuck River, although I would not try that now.

One of my favorite trips during the squirrel season—usually soon after the season opened the middle of August—was to a large stand of virgin timber called Becker's Woods, which was situated some three miles northwest of Crothersville if one went the route of the crow.

Here hickory, oak and yellow poplar trees more than three feet in diameter towered above beech, maple and a variety of other species, and the southeast side of the woods was bordered by an old riverbed, which was much too deep to wade in most places.

I would leave home at 2:30 or 3 o'clock in the morning and strike out over the paths and trails to the west until I came to a new road—appropriately named the Newcut Road because it was new and was cut through several big thickets. This road formed a T with the Retreat Road, which

I would follow to cross the Vernon Fork of the Muscatatuck before cutting through fields to the northwest and crossing the old riverbed on a logjam.

If I hustled I could be in Becker's Woods soon after daylight, and this would give me all morning and part of the afternoon to hunt, with time out for a siesta should the mood strike.

I liked Becker's Woods for several reasons. First, the squirrel hunting was always good there, but even if the hunting had been only so-so I probably would have spent a lot of time there for two other reasons. Size of the gigantic trees—one of the few stands of virgin timber I have seen in my life—undoubtedly was a strong force, but there was yet another reason.

At one point the woods dropped off into a bottomland a few hundred yards long, and here I discovered a number of sycamore trees that were six to eight feet in diameter. Some of these trees were hollow at ground level, and I soon learned that I could get inside them to escape rainstorms. The thought that I would have been in big trouble if lightning should strike one of these trees while I was inside never worried me.

I must confess, however, that a few times while I was sleeping through a prolonged rain I would dream that the passageway might grow together and I would be trapped.

I have told a number of people about these sycamores over the years and many, it was apparent, doubted my veracity. Can you imagine what they thought when I added that it was not unusual to find cow tracks inside the hollows of these big trees?

Across the old riverbed and due east from Becker's Woods there was a thicket of eight or ten acres on the west bank of the Muscatatuck's Vernon Fork, and interspersed were half a dozen or so large beech trees.

One of these trees was at least three feet in diameter

and was hollow from ground level up for quite a distance. This tree—like many beeches—was healthy enough, and there was a natural round hole large enough for a small boy to slip through about two and a half feet above the ground.

By leaning my rifle against the trunk of the tree either inside or outside, I could push my arms, head and shoulders through the opening and ease down inside the hollow. Getting my head and shoulders up again on the inside took some skillful moves, but I always made it in and out, especially if I was there when a storm was brewing.

This tree was situated at the edge of the thicket in such a manner as to offer an excellent view of the farm fields to the southwest.

Once while fishing the river on a hot August day I took refuge from a tremendous storm sweeping in from the southwest and was treated—though I was scared stiff at the time— to one of the most spectacular displays of lightning and thunder I have ever seen.

Jagged streaks of lightning came from high in the sky all the way to the earth, and gigantic claps of thunder rolled up and down the floodplain. The storm lasted for nearly an hour. I was glad when it was over, but I have thought many times since about the opportunity I had to observe that storm. Still, I would be reluctant to crawl back into that beech tree again today to view a replay.

One of my earliest recollections of napping in the woods came in Lou Nehrt's big bottom woods. It was not long after my dad turned me loose to hunt squirrels alone with the little rifle.

That woods was roughly two miles from Crothersville— which was about the limit of my range in the first year or two of hunting alone. The big thickets to the west and those northward on the Newcut Road beckoned, but I was more cautious then than I am now. I hunted the areas I knew best.

Actually, confining my efforts to Nehrt's Woods was not a bad plan because it gave me an opportunity to learn the location of the important trees in that woods and the other woodlots and thickets I would pass through on the way out and back home. It also explains why Nehrt's Woods and I became such friends.

My first experience at sleeping in the woods came on a hot August day when I had left home before daylight and cut through the fields and thickets on paths and wagon trails to get to the northeast corner of the bottom woods just about the time it got light enough to see my rifle sights.

I had hunted all morning without much success and climbed the hill on the south side of the woods about noon to find an apple tree at the edge of the woods, where I got my lunch.

After eating the apples I sat around the hill and watched some den trees for a while, but squirrels weren't moving much during the hot part of the day. I went back to the bottom woods, crossed the creek called the Hominy Ditch (because it served as a drain for the canning factory in town) and slipped back to the north side of the woods, where a large leaning hickory was being cut heavily by squirrels.

Earlier in the morning I had seen a squirrel leaving the tree before I got within shooting distance.

I checked the ground under the leaning hickory for fresh cuttings, but there were none, so I backed off and sat down with my back against a large beech tree and my body between two roots. It was almost like a big chair, the cover of dry leaves from the previous year making it a soft and comfortable place to sit.

"What the heck," I told myself, "I could wait for a squirrel to come to this tree through the hot hours of the afternoon, then start right there when the sun started dropping behind the thickets to the west."

In the meantime, I thought, if a squirrel should come to the tree during the hot part of the afternoon, I would be there and could shoot from my sitting position.

It worked out just the way I had planned it. But not quite. As the afternoon got hotter my body eased lower and lower in my natural chair between the beech roots, and before long my head was resting on the roots and my entire body was soothed by the soft carpet of dry leaves.

Sleep was inevitable. I fought it for a while, but each time I snapped my senses back to watching the hickory tree it required more effort to keep my eyes open. Eventually I surrendered. I was fast asleep.

I don't know how long I may have slept, but when I opened my eyes there was a squirrel on the ends of the beech limbs twenty or thirty feet above my head. The noise the squirrel made in jumping from one tree to another obviously had awakened me and now I was back in the squirrel hunting business.

The squirrel jumped from the beech to another small tree before I could scoot back up to a sitting position and get my hands on the little rifle. From there it jumped onto the leaning hickory and ran out to the end of a limb to get a hickory nut.

It went back to the trunk of the tree before starting to cut (eat) the nut and my seat offered a great view of the entire proceedings.

After rubbing the cobwebs out of my eyes, I silently cocked the rifle by depressing the trigger, pulling back the bolt, releasing the trigger and allowing the bolt to ease forward until it caught in cocked position. Then, from the classic sitting position, I lined the sights up on the squirrel's head and squeezed.

As I eased over to pick up the squirrel, I couldn't believe

how easy it had been. To make matters even better, I was refreshed from my nap and ready to start hunting again as the sun sank behind the thickets to the west, creating ideal hunting conditions.

In the years to come I would spend a lot of time both sitting and sleeping at that spot. It didn't always produce game, but it never failed to rejuvenate a tired body and mind.

One day a year or two later I was awakened from my slumber at this spot by a gentle tapping on the bottom of my shoes.

I awakened to find a big man with a shotgun towering above me, but I was startled only for a minute because I recognized the man as Hazel (Mike) Garriott, one of the older men who took me hunting occasionally.

"It's getting late," he said. "You'd better get up and get out of here. It's going to be dark before long."

Reluctantly I got up—I certainly didn't want to appear not to appreciate his concern—and slipped through the brush along the north side of the woods. Unfortunately, when I checked the forest floor under a little leaning hickory a hundred yards or so to the east, I found cuttings so fresh that moisture oozed out when I squeezed the pieces of nutshells. Obviously, the squirrel had seen or heard me and had stopped cutting momentarily.

My prescription for that situation was simple. I would back off to a little white oak tree a short distance from the hickory, sit down and be quiet for a few minutes—and I probably could get a shot at that squirrel.

For five minutes or so I craned my neck backward to look up at the hickory. When I saw no sign of the squirrel it became apparent that my neck would be more comfortable if I would slide down a bit. Z-Z-Z-Z-Z-Z-Z-Z!

I could not have been asleep more than a few minutes, but this time the tapping on the bottom of my feet was more forceful.

"I told you to get up and get out of here," Mike said. His voice was more forceful this time, too.

So I was up and away—headed out the east end of the woods even though Mike had offered to give me a ride to town if I would walk back to the west edge of the woods.

By now it was really late—probably too late to shoot a rifle in the woods with iron sights. But as I walked under another little hickory at the east end of the woods, there were cuttings on the ground so fresh they were still white.

I would sit down for just a short time, I told myself. I might get one more shot.

You know the rest of this story. I sat down, I scooted down to get more comfortable, and Mike pulled the chestnuts out of the fire for me one last time.

"I mean it this time," he bellowed. "You either get up and get out of this woods while I watch or you're coming with me."

I was convinced. But I still wonder what might have happened if it hadn't been so dark that I could not see cuttings on the ground as I passed under several hickories on the way home.

Of course, sleeping when you might otherwise be hunting or fishing has had its drawbacks for me. In that respect, at least, the practice of sleeping in the outdoors is like any other game—you win some and you lose some.

A couple of years back I was goose hunting at daylight on a rainy morning in December with Phil Hawkins and Nick Banos of Franklin and Ron Solt, the gridder.

We had set up well before daylight on a big farm pond south of Franklin in a driving rain with the hope that the weather would improve a little, but we were not getting our wish.

To further complicate matters, the birds had not moved out of Atterbury State Fish and Wildlife Area as they usually did soon after daylight. As a result, we kept getting wetter and colder by the minute. The night before I had gotten almost no sleep; little wonder that I should get one of my tremendous ideas about the time the rain seemed to be coming down even harder.

"Think I'll dry off a little in the old barn," I told them. Phil thought it would be the thing to do, too. So we mucked the fifty yards or so across the feedlot and slipped in out of the rain.

Phil went back to the blind a few minutes later when the rain slacked off, as I had fully intended to do. But in the interim I had noticed some perfectly inviting bales of straw. In a short time I had my rain gear fully zipped to capture and hold my body heat and I was drifting off.

I must have slept at least an hour, but I was awakened— and sat up to see and hear it all through the barn door—as a rollicking, gabbling flock of twenty-five or thirty big honkers fought the rain and wind across the picked cornfield and headed straight for our blind.

"Maybe," I told myself, as if I might have been dreaming, "the other guys came up to the barn, too."

But that was not the case. When the massive birds were twenty yards out, three shotgun barrels jabbed skyward from the blind and six birds—the limit for three hunters—fell before the shooting was done.

"Well," I thought, easing back down on the straw while closing my eyes, "at least I won't have to pick any birds tonight."

Some of My Best Friends
Were People

MR. TIPPECANOE

I THOUGHT OF A LOT OF THINGS as the windshield wipers
of the old pickup truck brushed aside the mixture of rain,
sleet and snow during the drive up the interstate to Monti-
cello late on a winter afternoon.

Lewis (Lou) Bowsher was the focal point of nearly every
thought, but this was only natural. I had known the colorful
man I had dubbed "Mr. Tippecanoe" for roughly thirty-five
of his ninety-three years, and soon we would be meeting
for the last time . . . in a funeral parlor. He would be buried
the next day at the town of Buffalo, his home for many
years, on the banks of the Tippecanoe River in White County.

I remembered the first thing he ever told me about fishing for smallmouth bass on his beloved Tippe: "Cast to the black bottom," he said. "That's where the smallmouth lives."

It didn't take long for me to realize that he knew of which he spoke.

But that was just the beginning. Lou taught me how to quarter a big yellow or black Heddon floater-diver River Runt on the surface of the riffles to drive bronzebacks stark raving mad, and how, when his antiquated reel started sounding like a coffee grinder, there was no oil so effective as the waters of his river.

"That ought to fix 'er," he would say, dipping his reel into the water over the side of his homemade jontype boat. Then he would rip off another cast in one smooth motion. It did "make 'er work," at least well enough for him to outfish everyone in the party on most occasions.

There were thoughts of Lou's dogs, Pluto, Cleo and Spike (the latter so well trained that he would bob for mussels in shallow water and put them in the boat). They all were of questionable ancestry, but he loved them with a quiet, almost obscure passion for what they were—highly valued friends and all-around hunters.

I hadn't made it to Lebanon before I remembered that summer morning when he pulled the boat to the banks of the Tippe and picked up his rifle, motioning me to come along.

"We'll have to be awful quiet," he said in a whisper as he told me how we would stalk the softshell turtles sunning on a sandbar downstream.

"Like an Indian?" I said.

"Nope!" he replied. "Quieter than that!" Then he explained that we would stalk the turtles as close as we could get and that he would shoot the biggest one of the bunch at a point on the back just above where the muscles of the front legs and neck are joined. This would paralyze the turtle and it would be unable to get back into the water.

In the next few minutes Lou put on a turtle-hunting clinic which would lead to a story for *Field & Stream* magazine and give this reporter a strong shove in the direction of becoming a free-lance writer, not to mention opening up another interesting outdoor activity.

I also remember Lou's thoughts on the longeared sunfish, the fish many anglers consider a trash fish but which is both one of the most beautiful fish found in Indiana waters and one of the tastiest.

"It's the best eating fish I know of," Lou would say emphatically when he would hoist a "redbelly" from beneath a log jam and put it in the live well of the boat, often throwing back larger fish of several other species.

There were those rainy winter days when we would come in from his trap line to fry big skillets of potatoes and onions and fresh-caught muskrat on hot plates in his fur house while talking for hours.

Lou guided and rented boats for float trips on the Tippe for many years from the first crack of spring into the fall. When he combined that with wintertime trapping and hunting, he didn't have much time left for any other kind of work.

"I wear out two pairs of hip boots a year," he used to say, a statement that spawned friendly envy in most of his customers and friends. Taking Lou a new pair of hip boots was like giving a chocoholic a two-pound Whitman Sampler.

One by one the hunting and fishing episodes we had shared over the years marched across my dashboard stage until I remembered a spring day when we were floating the river. I (as usual) was perched on the front seat where the fishing was always best. I got first crack at the best spots.

I hooked a big smallmouth—a five-pounder if it weighed an ounce—and had it on for what seemed like an eternity but probably was no more than a minute or two. The fish jumped and shook its head to send my single-hooked spinner-bucktail combination back at me as if to say: "Come back and try again any time, Sonny!"

Bemoaning this turn of events, I had some uncomplimentary things to say about that bronzebacked critter. Lou just laughed.

"She'll be there when we come down the river again," he said, and smiled—between chomps on the short cigar which almost always decorated the corner of his mouth. He let the current carry us on down the river.

It didn't make much difference what one wanted to do outdoors, Lou knew the whys, whens and wherefores of the game.

Once I called him late in the week to tell him I would be up the following Monday morning to accompany him on his trap line and maybe get some pictures. I arrived just after daylight on the appointed day.

A few miles out of Buffalo the back road ran parallel to a deep drainage ditch, and he stopped his dilapidated old pickup truck to check one of his sets.

"Sit tight," he said. "I'll take a quick look and call you if I have something."

A couple of minutes later he waved me down into the ditch to photograph the action as he took a mink out of his traps.

"I knew the light would be good for pictures here," he explained. "So I made that set yesterday afternoon."

The memories were great and I must admit that not all of the mist was on the windshield. Still, in the back of my mind I was bothered by something other than the fact that a good friend, a great Hoosier nimrod, was gone. I didn't know what it was, but something was bugging me.

Finally I knew about that too. As I walked slowly toward the casket at the funeral parlor to pay my last respects,

I realized that this was the first time I had ever seen Lou in a coat and tie.

It was a dark, rather formal coat and I couldn't keep from thinking that he looked as though he had just stepped off the page of one of those slick magazine ads you used to see touting men's attire in the *New Yorker* or *Esquire*.

Martha, his daughter-in-law, put things back into perspective for me, however, when she lifted the lapel of the coat to reveal a gold fishhook tie clasp.

On the road home again I had to smile as I remembered Lou's words on the one and only occasion he saw me in similar attire. It was a Sunday afternoon more than twenty years earlier when I knocked on his door unexpectedly. I was returning to Indianapolis from a weekend trip to a fishing tackle show in Chicago and had driven a little out of the way to stop and say hello.

Lou was a little bug-eyed at seeing me in that kind of getup.

"Sometimes," he said, shaking my hand and motioning me to a seat on the front porch, "an old muskrat looks pretty good if you put him in a fancy coat."

Amen!

MR. BUTLER

From his seat on the liars' bench outside Applegate's Grocery Store at Crothersville, Jack Cain used to say that if you would spin a milk bottle in the middle of the intersection of U.S. 31 and Howard Street and follow the direction it pointed when it quit spinning, you would find a covey of quail in a quarter of a mile or less.

I never doubted his word; he was my hunting and fishing mentor. Anyhow, there were too many houses in my hometown that had windows broken by flying quail.

It was a nice thing to contemplate when I was a boy,

but one thing not so nice to think about—especially on a beautiful Sunday afternoon in November 1941—was the fact that the bird season would open the next morning and I would have to be in school, certainly not hunting with Jack and the dropper (a cross of English setter and English pointer) named Duke.

As we sat on the liars' bench that Sunday afternoon Jack pointed out that a hunt together the next day would have added importance because he had been called to take his physical examination for the Army on Thursday of that week.

"It could be the last time we will be able to hunt together for a long time, Bill," he said. "If I pass the physical, I could be gone that day."

Jack was not asking—not even suggesting—that I play hooky. He wanted me to ask my dad if I could go.

As badly as I wanted to go, I told Jack it would be no use. My dad would not permit it, I was sure of that.

It would have been impossible to block the possibilities of a bird hunt completely out of my mind—I had seen Duke on point too many times and heard the whirr of too many bird wings, the "POW! POW!" of too many shotguns. But Jack's proposal was not mentioned at home on Sunday evening.

As I sat at the kitchen table having breakfast just after daylight the next morning, someone knocked at the kitchen door and I heard my mother tell someone to come on in, adding that I was having breakfast and getting ready to go to school.

You guessed it. It was Jack, and he poured out his tale of woe as my mother likewised him a cup of coffee.

By this time I had heard Jack's story so many times that I was almost willing to play hooky to go bird hunting, but my mother also knew where our bread was buttered. She told Jack she was sympathetic but she could not give me permission to stay out of school and my dad had already left for work.

"Well," said Jack after a few sips of coffee. "How would it be if Bill got dressed for bird hunting and we stopped at the school to get permission from Gene Butler (principal of the school)? If he says no there will still be plenty of time for Bill to come back home and change to school clothes."

My mother hemmed and hawed a bit at that, but finally agreed.

I was in knee boots and hunting togs in a matter of minutes. As Mr. Butler, the sternest but fairest educator I have ever known, pulled into the school parking lot, Jack and I were crossing the schoolyard toward the back door with shotguns under our arms and Duke tugging at his chain.

Jack held the guns and waited outside with Duke while I went to the second floor of the school and found Mr. Butler outside the study hall door. There I blurted out my spiel.

While I was telling the story and asking permission to go hunting with Jack, Mr. Butler's face got red, then livid, I fancied. I knew how David must have felt when he circled Goliath while searching for a vulnerable spot.

But when I was done and stood there shifting from one foot to the other, a smile crept across Mr. Butler's face and he decreed in the simplest of terms: "I can't tell you it's all right if you stay out of school and go hunting," he said. "But if you're not here today, I'll know where you are."

It was a great day. We found the first covey near the apple orchard just east of the school, but we didn't shoot them for two reasons. First, we almost always saved them for seed. Secondly, we didn't want to be shooting within earshot of the school.

We found more than enough birds in the Muscatatuck

River bottoms a couple of miles to the east. So many, in fact, that we both ran out of shotgun shells toward the end of the afternoon.

If the hunt was good, my return to school the next day was even better. Mr. Butler, still looking very stern, met me outside the study hall door again and handed me a signed note which said, still in the simplest of terms, that my absence from school the day before was "excused" and that I should be permitted to make up any schoolwork I had missed.

For some minor defect, Jack did not pass his physical and was on hand to take me on many more bird hunts before I enlisted in the Navy in February 1943. When I made it home on leave during the bird season, Jack always had a few boxes of shotgun shells in reserve for a hunt—no matter how hard they were to get.

It was a day and a pair of educators I will never forget.

ROSCOE (ROCKY) HAULK

I can't remember which of many high-powered creations it may have been, but on a February night a few years ago a bass fisherman stopped by the booth of the *Indianapolis Star* at the Indianapolis Boat, Sport and Travel Show to chat for a while.

"This any good for bass?" he said, fishing a goofy-looking contraption with two sets of treble hooks attached from a plastic bag.

I was tempted to tell him that the lure he had just purchased for the sports show sale price of $4.50 and a quarter of a stick of dynamite would get him all the fish he could carry.

But I didn't. Instead, as my mind wandered back nearly half a century, I laid the same words on the angler that Rocky Haulk, one of my best fishing friends ever, had hit me between the eyes with when I was a teenager.

"There isn't an artificial lure made that won't catch fish," I said, paraphrasing a statement Rocky used to make for my benefit when the fishing was slow and I got a bad case of "changeitis."

I would not have bet two cents that the angler asking me about the new bait he had just purchased would ever sink those hooks in the jaw of a bass, but I would have wagered a week's pay that it would have been a winner on Rocky's rod.

I had seen him take my cast-offs on too many occasions and turn them into the hottest thing on the Muscatatuck River, which we fished almost every weekend of the summer months and on into the fall. The old Muscatatuck has grown old with the rest of us, and it can now be considered nothing more than a semblance of the free-flowing stream it once was. But we both still fish it every time we get the chance—unfortunately we do not get to fish it together as often as we once did.

Rocky had an old tin boat which was light enough that the two of us could take it straight up over steep banks, log jams and other obstacles we would encounter on our storied float trips.

We rigged a kitchen chair (with short back) on the front seat of the boat and called it the "conning tower." One of us would sit in the conning tower to hit the best-looking spots with artificials while the other would sit in the back seat with short oars or homemade paddle to steer the boat.

Our unwritten rules provided that the fisherman on the oars also could fish so long as he kept the man in the conning tower in good places.

Thus, on Sunday mornings for sure—Saturday mornings, too, if Rocky didn't have to work—we would be off soon after daylight with a lunch sack large enough to have fed most of Morgan's Raiders and thermos jugs of coffee and lemonade. If it was late enough in the summer, a watermelon would be tethered to the back of the boat to chill in the river water, secured by a big fishhook in the stem and a strong cord tied to the rear seat.

Neither of us owned an automobile in those days. We would pay Clarence Koerner, a local painter, to take us to our starting point and pick us up somewhere else at dark.

Rocky was always strong on the Johnson Silver Minnow (spoon) with either Hawaiian Wiggler skirt or pork strips, but I was partial to the Jack's Dual Spinner, which was made nearby at Columbus.

We almost always would start with these lures, but during the day we would do a lot of experimenting with other baits, especially if the day grew hot and bright and the action slowed.

One such day stands out vividly in my mind, though, because Rocky demonstrated so well his theory that every artificial lure made will take fish if you'll give it a chance.

I was in the conning tower, but the day was hot, the sun bright, and neither of us had taken a fish for some time.

I kept cutting off lures and dropping them in the bottom of the boat behind me while complaining loud and long that we were just wasting our time being out there.

Finally I cut off a No. 1½ Hawaiian Wiggler with a red and white skirt and dropped it in the boat, and by this time Rocky had had enough of my pessimistic attitude.

"Hell, Bill," he said, picking up the discarded Hawaiian Wiggler and bending it onto his line, "there's not a bait made that won't catch fish if you give it a chance."

Before I could get another lure tied on and get fishing again, Rocky cast the lure in close to the roots of an old maple tree and soon was fighting a husky bass.

"See!" he said, emphasizing his point by holding the

fish high when I turned to see what was causing the commotion.

I didn't complain much after that about the lures I used. And when I changed lures, the discards were not strewn around the bottom of the boat.

Teenage boys will be teenage boys at times, and one of the times when I reverted from serious fisherman to nerd came on a day when I was floating the east fork of the Muscatatuck with Rocky. Although it was a Sunday and hunting was taboo, I had taken my little rifle along on this early October trip, thinking that I might also have the opportunity to bag a few fat fox squirrels.

Toward the middle of a beautiful sunny afternoon we were within half a mile of Wiesman's Ford, and since the fishing was slow I told Rocky I thought I would strike out on foot with my rifle for a while. I planned to rejoin him in the boat at Wiesman's Ford.

I didn't find any squirrels—or at least I did not get a shot—but on the high slate bank just before I got to the ford, there was a beautiful little cluster of trees that covered three or four acres and I decided that this would be a good place to wait for Rocky. There were all kinds of squirrel signs here, and I was certain I would get some shooting before Rocky came through the big deep hole seventy-five or a hundred feet below.

The shooting did not materialize, but as Rocky rounded a little bend and started through the long deep hole I was seized by this strange force.

I knew it was not the thing to do, but the ground was covered by these huge walnuts—larger than baseballs and soft and mushy on the outside. When Rocky drifted slowly into range, I started bombarding him with the walnuts.

I didn't hit Rocky, but the hail of walnuts ended any hopes he might have had for catching fish out of that hole of water.

I wasn't certain Rocky would stop for me at the ford—he was obviously pretty ruffled by my prank. But he pushed the bow of the boat in to the bank and I jumped back in the conning tower.

"Boys will be boys," he admonished me. "Now, let's get down to some serious fishing."